Caffeine Nig

The Fix

Keith Nixon

Fiction aimed at the heart
and the head...

Published by Caffeine Nights Publishing 2013

Copyright © Keith Nixon 2013

Keith Nixon has asserted his right under the Copyright, Designs and Patents Act 1998 to be identified as the author of this work

CONDITIONS OF SALE

All rights reserved. No part of this publication may be reproduced, stored in a retrieval system, or transmitted in any form or by any means, electronic, mechanical, photocopying, scanning, recording or otherwise, without the prior permission of the publisher

This book has been sold subject to the condition that it shall not, by way of trade or otherwise, be lent, resold, hired out, or otherwise circulated without the publisher's prior consent in any form of binding or cover other than that in which it is published and without a similar condition including this condition being imposed on the subsequent purchaser.

All characters in this publication are fictitious and any resemblance to real persons, living or dead is purely coincidental

Published in Great Britain by Caffeine Nights Publishing

www.caffeine-nights.com

British Library Cataloguing in Publication Data.
A CIP catalogue record for this book is available from the British Library

ISBN: 978-1-907565-41-0

Cover design by
Mark (Wills) Williams

Copy editor - Simon Jamieson
Original version cover image & design - Jim Divine

Everything else by
Default, Luck and Accident

Keith Nixon

Keith Nixon has been writing since he was a child. In fact some of his friends (& his wife) say he's never really grown up. Keith is currently gainfully employed in a sales role for a UK based high-tech company meaning he gets to use his one skill, talking too much. However he spends much of his time by the sea in a small town in the UK called Broadstairs where Charles Dickens briefly lived & was the inspiration for The 39 Steps.

For My Wife, Who Never Gives In

&

For My Grandparents, Wherever You Are

Author's Note

The events depicted in this novel won't be found in any official record, no matter how hard you search. Journalists, conspiracy theorists, the police and various other crackpot organisations have all tried and failed.

The crash of 2007 was like a house of cards tumbling, one taking down another. But it wasn't started by UBS. Not really. That's just what the pundits think, but they know nothing. Mine was the ace that, when drawn, started the banking collapse and financial difficulties the world has experienced for the last four years and counting. It wasn't a big card. In fact, it's one you'll never have heard of because of the cover-up. But sometimes that's all it takes – the lightest of touches, the faintest of breaths to bring everything down. And, as usual, it all comes down to money...

Prologue
Stone Cold (Almost)

I am fucked.

Unfortunately not in the sexual sense as even though I lie prostrate breathing heavily after an eruption of passion, it's not the blast of endorphins following an orgasm that courses through my veins.

No.

Life is, miserably, not that good to me. Never has been, never fucking will be. If I actually had the lack of good sense to believe in a God I would now know that he's a bastard who deliberately makes mere existence bloody complicated for the average you and me.

A few months ago I'd had it all. A (faithless) girlfriend, (shit) job, (asshole) boss and a career (founded on lies). In other words, material possessions and emotional wealth, perfectly fucking meaningless and of absolutely no use to me in my darkest hour. Even then, when I thought I believed life was adequate, I was already habitually, and unconsciously, perpetrating brainless errors. Conspiring with a cadaver is the final culmination of all those months of fuck-ups. If you believe in fate, this is it.

When I broke in minutes ago I was ready to kill my ex-boss, but — and it's a big but — somebody's got to him first. The guy I loathe more than anyone else in the world stares at me with wide, blank eyes that I no longer want to spit in. It'd be pointless really as he's stone dead, primarily because of a bloody great hole in the side of his head.

So I'm lying on my back with an exclusive view of an ornate ceiling. There's a stench of sweat, blood, cordite and fear. I'm breathing heavily. My heart is pounding. The room is dim, just a single lamp in the corner of the large room which stretches the shadows as if someone has pulled hard on one corner of the blackness. For a long moment I consider staying with the body, rotting with it. Nobody would miss either of us because nobody cares.

Then something persistently and annoyingly resilient nags at me, telling me to move. But I'm fucked, my synapses refuse to even glimmer, never mind combust. My mouth is dry, my body heavy, muscles atrophied and useless. My head is beginning to pound as alcohol poisoning kicks in. But like rubbing sticks together, eventually there's a little tinge of mental smoke as my mind catches slightly. I take my chance now. Before the glow fades I sit up, but my little world spins and I have to go horizontal again until everything stabilises. I try a second time, rolling onto my front like an asphyxiating fish on an angler's boat making a vaguely spirited attempt at escape from certain death.

My head starts banging even harder with the exertion. Deep breaths, then slowly I ascend onto my hands and knees to crawl a few feet, like an arthritic gerbil of perilously old age. The tangy metallic aroma of the blood is stronger next to the corpse. My gorge rises. I can taste stale beer and dry roasted peanuts, but I fight it back down. I assume the cops would be able to DNA-profile vomit and I really don't want to see the nuts again. They weren't that tasty the first time around, although the beer wasn't bad.

I slump back onto my haunches and study my deceased ex-boss. I'm no expert but suicide looks the most likely cause of his thoroughly deserved exit to the bank vault in the sky. There's a clutter of brain matter (which really is grey) and blood splattered all over the back of the leather wing back chair in which his corpse reclines. The stain darkens even as I stare in sickened fascination. His face is as vacant and vacuous as it was when he was breathing, but Hershey's eyes seem to look into mine with an abnormal intensity, like it's my fault he's dead. I wish it fucking was, but I'm pretty certain his demise ultimately has nothing to do with me.

Like my also late-departed sex life something is missing, but what? Then it hits my alcohol-soaked prune of a brain. Where's the gun? I'm pretty certain that a firearm is considered essential to propel a bullet into someone's brain. I look several times. There's nothing in his hand. The grand wing back has ornate legs that raise the base clear off the floor so it's easy to see there isn't a weapon on the floor or anywhere nearby.

I'm way out of my depth here. I need some help and bloody pronto. I scrabble to pull my phone out of my pocket, my hands shaking. I pause with a finger poised over the keypad, the screen bright. Was that a noise from within the flat? I listen hard but all I can hear is the thump-thump of my feathering heart.

The light on my phone goes out, the room dims again. I still need help. Automatically my finger moves to C, speed dial for Claire (arse score of 3, as I'll explain later). My trouser snake stirs with the memory of her, but then a cogent thought pokes through that's not my cock. I remember I'm supposed to hate her because she fucked someone who wasn't me. Anyway I deleted all her details from my phone and these days who bothers to memorise numbers? Certainly not me. I've a brief twinge of regret which I just as quickly squash like a fly.

Then a memory bubbles to the surface. The cops can triangulate phone positions, so I quickly dismantle my mobile, separating battery from handset. Time to get out of here. My mind urges me to move! Push up onto my feet, slight wobble, stabilise on thighs that ache from squatting too long, then lurch across the room without a backward glance, along the corridor and past the locked rooms. I realise the plush carpet deadens my footfalls (hysterical giggle at the word association). Down the stairs one at a time, lean on the wall for support. Turn left and through the front door. Out of the house and the relative cold hits me. It was so warm inside. Deep breath.

So here I am, back to the beginning of the end of my sad tale with a semi-erection that I really shouldn't have, a hangover and blood on my hands. I'd like to say it was a pity someone had to die, but I'd be lying.

It's only Hershey after all.

A Russian in Buenos Aires

A Couple of Months Earlier

There's a tramp who robs me every Wednesday, same time, same place. His name is Konstantin Boryakov and he claims to be an ex-KGB agent in hiding, afraid for his life because he pissed off some colleague years ago who subsequently became Russia's President and has a very long arm. I'm sure it's utter bollocks, but I'll let you debate it with him. Although his grey matted hair and beard is second to none and almost entirely hides his face, the guy stinks so much you can smell him a mile away, so keeping a low profile (the definition of being in hiding after all) is hardly a realistic option. No one in their right mind would want to go near Konstantin. Except me. For some reason I feel sorry for him. Fuck knows *why,* but I do.

Wednesday, early in the morning, late July and I'm walking to work, hurrying slightly as I'm a little behind time. The Russian doesn't like me to be tardy when he does me over. Places to be, people to mug, I assume. So I'm taking long strides along Margate seafront trying not to sweat too much. The air is still and close, barely a breeze off the sea. Although scientists claim a man's body odour is attractive to women I'm not convinced. To date I've found that reeking like a festering badger hasn't worked for either my sex life or my career.

It's not the most pleasant of routes either. To my right is a road that seems to carry sluggish cars and trucks whatever the time of the day. Beyond the clogged arterial thoroughfare is a wide strip of sand and then the North Sea, an expanse of muddy brown water dotted with massive ships heading in and out of the Thames. Beautiful it is not. To my left is Dreamland, the lurid amusement arcade which is alight with neon, flashing tubes and bulbs. It's a shabby throwback to yesteryear where the local chavs have always hung out. Great if you want some drugs or black-market Viagra. Not so great if you want to keep your watch, wallet or dignity. Walk quickly, look straight ahead and ignore the knock-off Burberry is my rule.

Which reminds me…The time. I flick a quick look at my watch. I'm definitely late. Fuck. I break into a trot which floats my tie over my shoulder like a hastily prepared hangman's noose. Past Dreamland, past Arlington House (another 1960's monstrosity, a high rise block of flats that leers over Margate like a rotten molar) and then into sight of the train station, which hunkers down and tries to hide from the locals on the far side of a busy roundabout. However, Konstantin likes to position himself away from the station, which frankly isn't a lot of use to me today when running behind schedule. Neither is being robbed, but I take my hurried chances with the traffic anyway, narrowly avoiding being crushed under the wheels of a Polish truck whose driver is more intent on ogling some blonde in a short skirt than looking out for errant pedestrians like me.

For a moment I consider some sort of protest. A shout like, "You fucking blind bastard!" springs to mind, but it's not the finest prose ever and the moment passes, as it does when the object of your derision is doing 40mph and possesses a mass of several tons.

Safely across, my would-be murderer in the lorry rumbling away into the distance, I can see the tramp standing in his customary location. Konstantin seems to find it highly amusing to wait for me and my wallet in Buenos Aires. Which, unfortunately, is not the vigorous Argentinean city, but an inexplicably named Victorian terraced cul-de-sac that nestles at ninety degrees to the sea adjacent to the roundabout whose teeming traffic had almost witnessed my untimely death. Maybe in the dim past this was indeed a vibrant section of Margate society, but those days are long, long gone.

I stroll over, walking along the axis of Buenos Aires. Konstantin, who stands on a dog-shit-peppered patch of grass, doesn't meet my eye. He doesn't acknowledge me at all, in fact. He likes to pretend we don't know each other, which is a lie because he's had lots of my easily earned cash (I work in a bank) in the last year. But the Russian also demands a challenge, a bit of drama in his misappropriation even though it's akin to a cat playing with a half dead mouse — the fight the expiring rodent puts up is minimal, but it's better than nothing.

One previous event illustrates this perfectly. After a few weeks of being voluntarily mugged I'd simply handed my wallet over when confronted by Konstantin. The Russian, swaddled in his threadbare hand-me-downs, had looked at the expensive piece of hand-crafted leather with disdain, turned his nose up and walked away without a word. I didn't lay eyes on the malodorous bum for several weeks, in fact I'd almost given up on him when, walking home one Tuesday evening after work, he'd popped up out of nowhere and scared the living shit out of me. He'd fixed me with a baleful, bleary-eyed stare and said, "See you tomorrow zasranec," and then shambled off. Normal service had clearly been resumed.

Back to now, and Konstantin moves to intercept me via a shuffling trajectory. He pays no attention to what's cluttering the grass and a rank smell explodes as he drags his feet through turds that have crusted over and festered in the heat. I stop in my tracks. So does he.

"Give your wallet, no shitty business," Konstantin husks and holds out his grubby paw, palm upwards, fingers curling like a claw.

My olfactory sense screams at me that the 'shitty business' is actually plastered all over his outsized shoes. "Why do I let you do this?" I say, asking myself as much as him — my first words to the tramp in all the time I've been allowing him to rob me.

The down-and-out Russian gives me a blank stare. His right arm is still outstretched but he crooks his index finger slightly in a 'come on' gesture. I'm clearly not going to get an answer so I pass over my wallet which he grasps before pushing it into a pocket in his stained coat, which was probably once green. I buy cheap canvas wallets these days. Although I can afford leather, as I earn far more money than my contribution to society justifies, the student buried in me still writhes at any unnecessary expense.

With his left hand Konstantin simultaneously returns the empty wallet he had appropriated last week and then twists away to reposition himself on the grass/shit strip. I'm about to speak again, but the squealing sound of metal on metal that is a train slowing down intrudes and the query is lost forever.

I turn and bolt.

A Wolf in Lamb's Clothing

Life.

It's like a snow globe. From the outside it can look pretty, idyllic, calm. But in reality it's a sham. Look closely inside and you'll see everything is fake, plastic, very small and very, very meaningless. And then every now and again some bastard comes along and shakes the whole lot up. Which was Mr Lamb's job and he excelled at it.

Mr Lamb had the most inappropriate surname in the history of the human race. He wasn't soft, he wasn't cuddly, he didn't bleat and it was usually Mr Lamb that did the slaughtering (but in a metaphorical sense, he would insist if pressed). He was truly devoid of emotion and (he thought) utterly empty-hearted. Along with a tack-sharp intellect, these attributes meant he was very, very focused on whatever task was at hand and the task at hand right now was one Josh Dedman.

So far Dedman had been exactly the opposite of a puzzle — as transparent as glass and with the stimulation equivalent to a Sun crossword puzzle (he was a Sudoku fanatic from his time in Japan). Mr Lamb mentally ticked off what he had learned so far

1. *Dedman had an entirely uneventful personal life.*
2. *His only meaningful human contact was with a relatively plain girlfriend who was difficult to like. He appeared to have no other friends to speak of.*
3. *He had no family in the immediate area.*
4. *He was unfortunate enough to reside in a dead end, shithole of a town that Mr Lamb hoped he never had the misfortune to return to once his assignment was over.*

Based on these observations Mr Lamb would ordinarily have concluded that Dedman was hardly the perpetrator of the major crime of which he was suspected. But two things kept him on Josh's trail.

First was his most recent observation from where he was seated in the back of a taxi. The robbery that wasn't jarred with him. Unexplained data always niggled at Mr Lamb; he didn't like things that wouldn't fit in a neat symmetry. He liked his conclusions to be clear because there was no room for grey in his life. Grey got you killed.

Second, he was far too experienced (and sceptical) to make a snap judgement. A week of following someone around was hardly long enough to know everything about them, particularly the clever ones. He had to concede that Dedman, although somewhat dull, wasn't stupid.

He folded up the deceptively small but powerful binoculars and placed them into the briefcase next to him. Then he leant over to the taxi driver, an Indian wearing an impressive turban and with more than a hint of curry on his breath. "Station, please," Mr Lamb murmured, barely above a whisper.

He like peace and calm in his life. He detested loud people in loud situations who, it always seemed to him, were simply stating, 'Look at me!' Mr Lamb liked people to look in the opposite direction, not at him.

The taxi driver jerked a nod at the instruction and put the car into gear. He hoped his passenger was leaving. Something about the man bothered him greatly. Maybe it was the bible-black eyes.

The taxi cut into a slot in the traffic and flowed around the roundabout like a turd in a u-bend. Moments later the driver nosed into the train station entrance. Dedman dashed past at that point and Mr Lamb turned his head away, just in case he glanced in. But the precaution was unnecessary; Dedman was too intent on making the train.

"Here will do fine, thank you," he stated politely and pressed a crisp £20 note into the driver's hand, appropriated his briefcase and slid out of the car in one smooth movement. Barely had he pushed the door shut when the taxi squealed away.

But Mr Lamb did not notice the Indian's rapid exodus. His eyes were fixed on Dedman's rear, which was diminishing at a comparatively sluggish rate. He struck up an ambling pace, sufficient to follow at a measured distance. Ultimately, even if Dedman had been travelling at the speed of sound, there was no rush as he knew Josh's precise destination, because he was employed by the same corporation. No need to buy a ticket either, he'd a season ticket for the duration. As the train sidled up to the platform with a squeal of rusted brakes on worn wheels he watched Dedman bend over double, hopelessly out of breath after such a pathetically short lope. Once stationary, only the conductor bothered to step off the train (passengers rarely did, why would they?) so Mr Lamb had to twist the handle and tug open the door to the ancient carriage himself.

Inside, the seating comprised rows of benches perpendicular to the windows and separated by a narrow corridor which united doors at either end of the carriage. Mr Lamb had found a surprisingly large proportion of old slam-door trains in service on the South Eastern line during his time going back and forth to the capital. The majority of his fellow passengers moaned about them, but he quite liked the nostalgia they invoked in him (an emotion which surprised him greatly). However, he knew he wasn't doomed to spend nearly two hours on a knackered old train twice a day for the rest of his life...

He sat down in a carefully selected location, able to see Dedman as a reflection but largely out of sight himself. He pulled The Times out of his briefcase as extra insurance. He lamented the loss of the broadsheet style, but grudgingly conceded that overall the smaller format was more convenient for handling yet would still satisfactorily mask his features should the need arise. He flicked through the paper, found the puzzle section, and then settled back, pen poised, as the train pulled away with a slight lurch. He had plenty to consider besides the immediately obvious answer to the Sudoku quiz.

Strangers On A Train

The carriage is pretty much empty. I live out in the sticks and not many people board before me, so as usual I've got plenty of choice where to park my arse. Feeling somewhat sorry for myself, and in need of reparation, I decide to flop down on an entirely empty row. I'm knackered and still out of breath — despite all the walking I incur around London I must admit I'm not particularly athletic. The other keep-fit routine most men of my age (29) seem to constantly undertake, if the conversations I hear are to be believed, is something Claire is uninterested in.

I'm talking about shagging of course. Claire and I have been together since university. These days we very seldom rub our erogenous zones together for mutual pleasure, and whenever I think about this sad fact (with abject distress) I draw the conclusion that it can only result from the over familiarity arising from spending eight years with the same person, poking the same hole(s) in the same position(s). This is what I tell myself.

In my hardly enlightened opinion the Achilles heel of the average male isn't actually their, well, Achilles tendon, but their cock. So I give you a scientific fact — everything a man does is driven by obtaining the maximum satisfaction of their genital region. And I, unfortunately, am no different. This fact leads to the one absolutely impossible challenge that has been attempted by man since the dawn of time, back (if you believe in all that religious bollocks) to Adam trying it on with Eve on a Saturday night after five pints down the pub with his mates and then having a row about it with her before slinking off with a hangover and unfulfilled lust.

As Adam found — and must have called God a twat as a result (although we've already established God is a figment of imagination) — a man *cannot* win an argument with a woman when sex is involved. It's a universal rule, as fundamental as gravitational theory. Scientists (the bastards) have recently proved that women require orgasms at much lower frequency then men — in other words they can abstain for longer, severely limiting any male's ability to succeed in gaining the upper hand. Going AWOL (Absent WithOut Libido) doesn't work, neither does having a quick shuffle in the shower which, from personal experience, is only fulfilling for as long as it takes to dry off.

Therefore it is a *guarantee* that you'll crack before they do, you *will* collapse and apologise for anything, *anything* just to get your girlfriend to spread her legs again. Like a prisoner in an Iraqi prison, you'll sing a confession to all sorts of crimes you had no idea you'd committed until that moment of clarity. And then, when she does drop her drawers, guess who gets the most out of it? Correct, Einstein — women's orgasms last longer than men's, which is another scientific fact. I ask you, where's the fucking justice in *that*?

Anyway, last night Claire and I had had yet another argument, yet again a heated debate over Konstantin. She struggles to understand why I repeatedly subject myself to the self-inflicted mugging process every week. As we'd sat simmering in a soup of resentment, the ingredients comprising anger (her) and sexual frustration (moi), it dawned on me that a shag was absolutely out of the question (again). Nevertheless I tried it on, we rowed, she left claiming I was 'pressurising' her, I went to bed frustrated, barely slept, got up, got robbed and boarded the train. A typical 24 hours in my hugely unsatisfactory life.

The fact is *I* can't fucking understand my motives when it comes to Konstantin, and of course this is something I don't want to admit to Claire (another rule: never volunteer any information to a woman, unless you want it to come back and bite you on the arse at some point in the future).

With Claire in mind I tug my Blackberry out of my jacket pocket and press the C key. The number dials rapidly and connects within seconds. But the ring tone continues until voicemail kicks in. "This is Claire Pigeon," says the recorded message. "I'm not available right now so make your point after the tone...unless it's Josh to whom I say, Don't bother, fuck right off."

That's telling me, so I end the call with a heavy sigh. It's odd. These days the smallest of things irritate both of us. Events or comments that we laughed at only months ago now inflame us into blazing rows or seething antipathy. All of which is forcing me to look at Claire in a very different light.

I've known for a long time that she utterly isn't my type — tall, slim, relatively flat-chested (a poor A cup at best), mousy hair and a rare applicator of make-up. Not that I like a girl who plasters foundation on like an Irish navvy, but on the other hand neither do I see anything wrong with a bit of positive enhancement of the facial region. In addition I've recently begun to look at other girls, something I've never done previously in our time together. You know what my conclusion is? *All* the ones that catch my eye appear more attractive than Claire. Much more attractive (except the bloaters).

The train lurches forwards, tugging on my carriage as if it is on a piece of unrepentant knicker elastic that at first stretches then regains its tension with a jerk. A man flops down on the seat opposite me, thrown there by the action of the train driver.

"Mornin'," he says, sickeningly cheerful and with a serious flashing of pearlies.

Great, I think, fighting the natural inclination of my face to smile back politely because it only encourages idiots like this. I curse my rotten luck. An entirely empty carriage and Mr Positive ends up opposite me, and is clearly a talker, just the antithesis of what I need in my current monumentally confused disposition.

"Jack Dean," he says in reaction to the smile my mouth has betrayed me with. He wipes his palm on his trouser leg before holding it out for me to take.

"Hi," I say grudgingly, not willing to swap my identity with him just yet. But my polite upbringing overpowers my sense of judgement and I accept the handshake. He tries to crush my fingers in a show of superiority which reinforces my first impression. An overtly strong grip just makes me think the guy (or woman, let's not be sexist) wanks a lot, and on the evidence Jack must be pre-eminent in masturbatory society.

As he releases my hand I give him a quick glance over. Jack is clad in a sharp, dark blue suit paired with a crisp white shirt and neatly folded tie. His black hair is slicked back, but betrays a slight natural wave, and there's a strong aroma of aftershave sluicing off him. Smart, but everything is just a little *too* well done — the shirt collar large, the tie bright with a knot you could secure a boat with and the teeth in his cheesy grin as white as the chalky cliffs of Dover. He's the modern day image of an 80's yuppie. If he produces a Filofax in the next few seconds I swear I'll batter him to death with it and gladly admit my guilt to the cops, secure in the knowledge they'll never find a jury to convict me.

"Going to the Big Smoke?" Jack smiles, again exposing sparkling enamel capable of taking my eye out at twenty paces.

"Uh-huh." Now I can reply with deliberate rudeness because my courteous nature has slunk off to a corner in abject defeat. I even look out the window at the houses crawling past as we slowly pick up speed. The journey is almost two hours long and I cannot face an interminable conversation with someone like Jack. However, there is hope. At the next stop, only minutes away, it's typical that a multitude will board so it's possible Jack will target a more willing sucker. Or fuck off. Either is fine with me.

"Me too," he continues. "Big, important meeting with some, uh, important types."

"Sounds…important." Fucking hell, I cringe. It's like something out of a sitcom as outmoded as Jack's dress sense.

"I've seen you on here a few times. Do you go up every day?"

"Uh-huh."

"Work in the City?" he asks.

Words fail me so I nod. Brain surgeon clearly isn't his, uh, important role.

"What do you do?" Jack asks. He's starting to struggle, I notice with relief.

"Nothing significant."

Jack laughs. "Everything's significant! Particularly if it makes oodles of dosh for people, me specifically."

Surprisingly Jack hits the nail on the head (even a blind carpenter achieves that feat every now and again — think monkeys, typing and Shakespeare). I've struggled with this particular concept quite a few times, and more often recently. What *do* I really do? I push a pen (more accurately a mouse) in a decent-sized investment bank. I sit in meetings and I make presentations. My job does indeed create (more accurately facilitate) wealth, lots of it, most of which is siphoned off by the Culpeppers, the family that has owned the Bank for generations. Sure, I can put up with my job, but it doesn't add value to society, it doesn't make a real *difference* to anyone's life. Nobody lives, nobody dies as a by-product of my decisions. So, by extension, I don't make a difference to anyone.

"Fucking hell, that's depressing," Jack says, grimacing. He looks disgusted with me, as if he's eaten something that disagrees with him and just brought a little bit of sick into his throat.

With a jolt I realise I've been talking out loud but, equally surprising, I'm not actually bothered by his look of revulsion. Before he gets the chance to act all superior the train pulls into Broadstairs station and Jack's attention wanders. In moments doors all along the carriage are yanked open and people in droves breeze in as I had hoped.

Although doors slam shut again one after the other with the vigour of a starter's pistol, no one sits near us. My heart sinks as Jack grins at me. Then a body enters my peripheral vision. A stunningly beautiful woman (arse score 9.5). She slides along the bench, torso twisted away, presses herself up against the window and looks out of it. Even in that merest glance I can see she's a striking blonde, good legs, conservatively dressed. *One of the relocated London set*, I think. Nice big sparkler and wedding band on the right (or wrong depending upon your perspective) finger confirms it — too expensive to be a local. There are an increasing number of them moving down to breathe the clean sea air with the promise of a fast rail link that has yet to arrive.

The blonde glances at her fingers, as if checking the quality of a recent manicure. Then she slips the rings off and places them into her handbag, a Radley judging by the little leather cut-out dog emblem that hangs from the handle. She glances over, sees Jack and me taking her in and instantly colours. Jack shakes his head slightly. Then a ringtone emits from the blonde's handbag. She pulls out a mobile, looks at the number and swears under her breath. She answers, turning her back on us. Jack maintains his attention on unfortunate little me and I can tell it's going to be the longest journey since man invented iron, the wheel or maybe even fire.

What had I done to deserve this?

Who had I murdered in a past life?

Who could I murder in this one to escape?!

Finch

"I told you, I'm on a day off," Serena complained. She kept her voice down so no one could overhear her, particularly the suit across the way. Part of her brain was still rattling with being seen removing her rings. Another brick in her wall of deceit.

The people on the train were in effect her neighbours and her husband was a wealthy man. She couldn't risk her status and the quality of life she was used to. However, there were other...stimulants that a woman like her needed and simply couldn't do without, no matter what the risk to her lifestyle.

"Look love, all I'm asking you to do is shag someone on camera, not commit murder," said the man on the other end of the line, her agent Julius Finch.

"I'm well aware of what you're asking and I'm telling you I *can't* today," Serena hissed.

"Got the decorators in?"

"Crudely put, but yes. In fact a whole team of them for major reconstruction work," Serena said, relieved to have been given an excuse her temporarily flummoxed brain was unable to deliver by itself.

"No problem," Finch replied, unswayed. "All blowjobs or some anal will do just as nicely, maybe even better perhaps. No need for our guy to get his cock bloody. Costs more."

"Look my...," Serena had to think at a lower and coarser echelon than she was used to in order to deal with Finch, "twat is in a right state. It looks like a battered piece of sirloin."

"Some men love that kind of thing. Like me for instance," Finch sniggered.

Serena shuddered. "Anyway, I'm not legal yet."

"You looked over 18 to me," Finch sounded puzzled. "In fact you looked a lot older. Maybe even into MILF territory."

"Thanks for the compliment Julius. What I mean is I haven't got my performer's licence yet. We wouldn't want to see you disbarred now, would we?"

"Shit," Finch said, putting the weight of nations behind his exclamation. "All right, I'll have to find someone else. Opportunities to make a film like this don't come knocking on my door very often."

"Couple of days and I'm all yours. I promise."

Finch audibly sucked his breath in and then to her surprise the connection was abruptly cut. It sounded like he'd dropped the receiver. Serena powered down her phone entirely so Finch couldn't call her back and returned it to her bag.

She looked around. The two suits were staring at her, one open-mouthed, the other shaking his head. Serena cringed, she could do without being judged again by him. Perhaps she hadn't spoken *quite* as softly as she'd thought and a fresh wave of guilt caught her, mentally bowling her over once more. She dragged her gaze away from her conscience and caught the eye of a good-looking guy who was placing his briefcase on the rack above his seat. He winked. She smiled. He smirked.

The guilt was nudged away as Serena's beam stretched down to her sirloin steak and it flooded her body with hormones.

Hello

As soon as the blonde ends her call she turns away from us and buries her head in a girlie mag. You know the ones. Bright, glossy and stuffed with the sort of 'celebrity' gossip that when your girlfriend offers it to you, you decry it as a piece of crap. Yet when she's out of the room you're drawn to it as inexorably as light to a black hole, so you pick it up and read it from cover to cover, even wondering if Skinny Beckham does look good in a pair of jeans that cost the same as the average family spends on food in a month. Then, a couple of days later, she *knows* you've read it because you unwittingly repeat during a lull in conversation, ad infinitum, a soupcon of scandal that you, as a male, cannot possibly know from anywhere else but that selfsame fucking magazine. What kills me is her knowing smirk, the smug nod that acknowledges my life is richer thanks to her crappy, waste-of-space magazine.

"I'd like to meet one of these so-called nym-pho-maniacs," drones Jack, stretching out the word like it was a convoluted name for some virulent disease. He nods at the blonde's glossy publication. "But I don't believe they exist, they're a cruel myth."

He looks at me for affirmation. I'm staring out the window at fluffy sheep, but he continues anyway. "I had a mate once. Every girlfriend he had was a nympho and he hated it. Apparently one used to wait up every night for him to come up to bed. He'd hide in the shed, garage or pub until it was late enough that she'd get bored and go to sleep. What an idiot. My mate had a wife's approach to sex — once a week was enough for him, so where's the justice in him pulling nymphos?"

I look up and he grins at me, assuming I'm actually interested in his shitty drivel. He chitters away like this for what seems hours.

"Which reminds me, I haven't given you my contact details yet," he says.

He reaches into his inside pocket. It's pretty unlikely he's going to give me money so — Oh God (even though I don't believe in you) — it must be the dreaded *business card*.

It is, and what an example. It's black with a sheen that'll melt your face off if you stare at it for too long, overlaid with gold embossed lettering, like you see on a tombstone. Jack hands over the vile tome reverentially, as if he only gives them out to the honoured few. Like the earlier handshake I reach out involuntarily and take the card. I read it:

Jack Dean
Executive Business Consultant

There's a telephone number underneath, but no address.

"Turn it over," Jack urges.

On the reverse, in gold again, are Chinese letters in the same arrangement with an identical telephone number underneath.

"I went international a few years ago. Great business in China. You should go there, they do a mean Peking duck."

The blonde chooses that moment to exit, taking her bag but leaving behind the magazine which looks hardly touched. Someone is in her seat before the springs have had a chance to relax. No prisoners in this game. Jack watches her melt into the standing crowd, a frown creasing his crown.

"Can I get yours?" Jack asks when he returns his attention to me, but he looks and sounds distracted.

"My what?" I'm still dumbfounded with the tackiness of his card. The girly gossip mag suddenly looks decidedly upmarket in comparison.

"Your business card."

I've clearly succumbed to a degenerative brain disease because I stupidly hand over my far more austere example. Jack takes it, skims it quickly and puts it away, probably to mate with his own and produce a litter of mongrel business cards.

"I'll give you a call some time," he says glancing up as a man pushes through the crowd in the blonde's wake.

I grin with my teeth whilst I die inside just a little more.

Jack stands up then and says, "I need the bog."

Illicit Encounters

Serena couldn't contain herself any longer. She'd desperately been trying to focus on the magazine, but had utterly failed. She could feel his eyes roving all over her body again, the good-looking one a few rows down, the walking (but currently seated) cock. Every time she peeked up he looked straight back at her, a tickle of a smile ghosting his lips. Typically men would glance away before she could meet their eyes, in a pretence that they hadn't been staring at her. But not this one. He was a handsome bastard and knew it full well.

Minutes ago, when a space became vacant, he'd relocated from the window to the corridor end of the bench with the sole intent of being better able to ogle her legs and tits. She knew this because his gaze was open, obvious and without the merest hint of embarrassment. He wore a wedding ring, a thick, evident gold band. But he didn't seem to care about his marital status and frankly, neither did Serena. She knew it was wrong, knew she would hate herself the instant after he pulled out, but she just couldn't help it.

Because she had one fundamental problem in life. Although her husband earned plenty of money he simply hadn't fucked her enough, but then no man could. He'd also been a pretty dull and unimaginative partner, permanently tired or recovering after extended hours in the office. On the rare occasions Serena had coaxed enough life into James's cock with a long blowjob she'd usually ended up climbing on top for, if she'd been lucky, a whole two minutes. Enough time for him to find release, but utterly pointless for her, who'd barely got going.

Then he'd come out and all had made sense.

So Serena had started to look elsewhere for satisfaction and quickly found she could obtain it whenever and wherever she wanted. To be frank, what woman couldn't if she put her mind to it? Men are always willing participants. Any lingering doubts that she'd had about her extramarital activities were soon pushed to the back of her mind, vaginal instincts surging to the forefront. As Serena didn't work (being fully provided for by her hard-working husband) she could fuck other people several times a day if she wanted. However, because the sex was readily available, even this had become boring and she needed to look for ever-increasing thrills and bigger risks to get off. And now here she was.

Serena glanced at her watch. About 20 minutes before they arrived at Kings Cross. Long enough to get what she wanted, too long to resist even though she knew she really should because within the hour some doctor would be probing her internal passages. Serena made up her weak mind, fixed her soon-to-be encounter with a firm and meaningful look, then stood up. She threaded her way through the people standing in the corridor and past him, lightly touching his shoulder as they crossed, just in case he'd missed the most obvious of hints.

When she reached the toilet she glanced over her shoulder and saw handsome guy coming towards her, a huge and soon-to-be-satisfied grin stitched on his face. Serena almost turned away then, but the urges had too hard a hold of her. She steeled herself, entered the stall and awaited his knock, which couldn't come fast enough.

Jack elbowed his way to the toilet. People were getting out of the way far too slowly in comparison to his needs so he decided a more direct approach was needed.

"Can you shift it love, I'm busting for a shit here," he said to an ancient woman who must have at least been in her forties. She stepped back a pace, aghast.

He reached the toilet, too late. The sign said engaged. He swore and tried the handle anyway, rattling it vigorously. It didn't budge. *Of all the fucking luck*, he thought.

"Emergency! Man about to explode in his pants out here!" Jack shouted, banging his fist on the door in vain hope.

Serena wished the man in her would explode too. She'd opened the door at Handsome Guy's urgent knock and stepped back as he slid through the crack, pushing it to behind him. Handsome Guy turned and locked the door again, then went straight for her tits. Men, she knew, were divided into those who were tit-fixated (and had usually been breast-fed as babies) or arse-obsessed (no idea what they'd been brought up on!) with about a two-thirds, one-third split respectively from her quite extensive analysis. Sometimes you got both (i.e. men with hands that could act independently) but that was much rarer as it implied he could do two things at once.

After yanking open her top and spilling her breasts out of her bra Handsome Guy had gone straight for the kill, turning Serena around, pushing her head down (fortunately the toilet lid was closed) and pulling up her skirt in one swift movement. Her knickers proved only a minor impediment and she grinned and grimaced at the same time as she heard and felt the rip of lace.

Without any preamble he slid inside (fortunately she was already wet from trying to fight her inner urges) and began banging away. And banging away. And banging away. Serena looked pointedly at her watch, only five minutes before the train arrived. The pumping suddenly speeded up for a few seconds and then abruptly stopped. One last jerk and he pulled out.

"That was cool," Handsome Guy said.

Serena turned around, and found him already zipped up and ready to go.

"See you again," he said insincerely, unlocked the door, opened it wide this time, and stepped outside. Serena saw a face in the corridor, barely a smudge of shock, before she pushed the door to and locked it. That was it. She wasn't even sure she'd had an orgasm. She looked down at her torn knickers discarded in a shambolic heap on the floor and already the guilt and shame were hitting her as hard the guy's hips had pounded her pelvic bone only moments before. She picked up the decimated underwear, ran them under the tap, rinsed the excess water out of the material, then cleaned herself up before finally drying off her pussy with a couple of rough paper towels that did her bruised lips no good at all.

Practical issues dealt with she flopped down onto the toilet. At that moment she hated her vagina, wished she could scream for a surgeon and have it amputated there and then, the amount of trouble it caused her. Probably Handsome Guy was already laughing with his mates about the tart he'd just shagged. And that's what she felt like. A slapper, completely out of control. Driven by urges one minute, eaten up by them the next.

She felt the train slowing, heard the intermittent squeal of brakes as they were applied. She checked her watch. The train was late (as usual) but she couldn't face exiting into the tangle of people outside the toilet who must have heard her antics, so she resolved to wait for a few minutes after the train stopped. But it couldn't be much longer, otherwise she'd miss her appointment.

Jack was also, finally, in a toilet, but he was flying solo. Trousers around his ankles he had decided to have a quick wank after the very satisfying and odorous dump he had delivered. He figured a five-finger (strictly four fingers and a thumb) shuffle was acceptable as no one would want to come in and smell the brown roses anyway. Almost done and toilet paper ready to catch his ejaculation, he felt the jerk of the train as it pulled into the station. The sudden movement completely threw him of his stride.

He then experienced the familiar feeling all men have had of interrupted self-pleasure. As this usually occurs when the wife or girlfriend enters the bathroom uninvited (then quickly leaves in disgust) it was not something Jack was used to as he'd never had the pleasure (literally) of a girlfriend.

He tried to tug some life back into his cock, but it sagged all the more under the pressure to perform in the now difficult and focused circumstances. He sighed and admitted defeat. He pulled his trousers up and notched his belt whilst he listened at the door. He couldn't hear any movement out there so he slid back the bolt and sidled out. Thankfully the corridor was empty. He stepped off the train in the manner he imagined dirty old men in raincoats who didn't want to be identified departed brothels. Looking up the platform towards the exit he fancied he recognised that bloke Josh he'd been talking to earlier. He called out his name whilst breaking into a loping gait in an attempt to track the banker down, but in the swollen exodus Jack quickly lost sight of his newfound friend.

Run Forrest!

When I finally manage to get off the train the crowd is almost gone, moving, as they always seem to, like water gurgling down a plug hole in a whirling, churning confusing mass of identical, anonymous bodies. As I don't much like being in the press of my fellow man (although I am not so upset about the press of fellow woman) I always aim to be on the periphery of the flood, at either the fore or rear. On this occasion I hang back in the hope that my newborn friend has taken his dubious relationship, and dress sense, elsewhere. On the platform a breeze blows, funnelled by the contour of the station itself. Rubbish twirls in a mini cyclone. There's already the odour of exhaust fumes and people, a change I never really get used to after the freshly-salted sea air of home.

My delay proves to be a decent call (a rare event it transpires) as the blonde steps off a couple of carriages in front of me, the first I've seen of her in half an hour or so. She is quite cute, although the flustered, red-faced expression that chases across her features doesn't do her any favours. She stuffs something looking suspiciously like a pair of knickers into her handbag, albeit shredded and dirty. Without seeing me she strides away. Ah well, ships that pass in the night and all that.

I follow in her wake (not stalk, by the way) at a somewhat slower pace. I'm in the process of pulling out my exorbitantly expensive travel card to flash at the guard manning the barrier when I freeze inside. Someone has shouted my name and it's not hard to guess who. I hunch my shoulders, present my pass and get out as quickly as I can. No fucking way am I going to reveal to Jack where I work.

As another shout rips through the air I break into a run. Body odour be damned.

I Love Me

Hershey Valentine was in love. The object of his affection (Hershey, of course) grinned back at him in the mirror. He washed the razor in the sink and scraped another line of foam away, the rasp audible as it traversed over his square chin. A few more scrapes, a quick rinse with cold water and the job was complete. He opened a cupboard, winking at himself again in the mirror as he did so, then applied some aftershave balm, allowed it to dry and followed up with a disrespectfully obvious cologne.

Hershey had expensive tastes which his bathroom, in fact his entire house, reflected perfectly. Every item was branded and top of the range, the primary selection criterion being affluence. Marble, imported at great cost from Europe to replace the previous (and already opulent) materials used in the bathroom, stretched from floor (Italian) to ceiling (Spanish). He had Jack and Jill sinks (although there was no official 'Jill' in his life), a toilet, roll-top bath, shower and bidet (used even less than the Jill sink, but Hershey thought it looked cosmopolitan and would impress his dinner guests as they tried to guess its purpose).

After one last admiring glance in the mirror Hershey exited the bathroom, a towel (Egyptian cotton) wrapped around his waist. A hop across the landing and he was in his bedroom. There was a hump in the middle of the expansive bed that dominated the space, a girl he had humped (he laughed to himself) last night. On the bedside cabinet was an ice bucket half full of tepid water and an upturned champagne bottle. Christ knew where the crystal glasses had ended up.

He began to dress, not bothered at all whether he disturbed the tart. With a hint of OCD he had neatly laid today's clothes out the previous evening. His attire didn't include underwear, as Hershey liked to go commando, but did comprise socks (with garters), trousers (crisply pressed), a shirt (monogrammed) and a jacket (Saville Row). After the trousers and shirt were in place he snapped on braces (à la Wall Street) then fumbled with cufflinks (gold dollar signs) and a tie. He shrugged on the matching jacket, pushed a fat wallet into an inside pocket and a gold watch onto his right wrist, turning the face around so it was palm side down. Hershey liked to make a big show of checking the time; he was a man that impressed himself, and therefore others, on a frequent basis.

"Let yourself out," he said to the hump (he laughed to himself again). No response. Hershey hated a lack of feedback from those he abused. "Use whatever you want but don't blag anything — I know where you work, Elodie."

He trotted down two flights of stairs, pausing briefly by the front door to pick up car keys, house keys and his all-bling, no-bang cell phone from where they nestled on a Louis XIVth cabinet (unknown to Hershey it wasn't French at all, but made in Dagenham by the finest late 20th century crooks). A blinking ruby red light on his phone piqued his attention because it meant a new communication. Hershey liked to pick up his e-mail outside hours as it made him look like the committed, hard worker that he actually wasn't. The e-mails from the few people in the Bank more senior than him took priority, of course. However, when he read the note his face darkened.

"For fuck's sake," Hershey barked and immediately banged out a reply.

For all his bullying bluster Hershey preferred indirect confrontation, unless he had a cast-iron case and utter superiority, so an electronic reply was perfect to deal with the sales woman that kept vying for his business, which he categorically didn't want to give. Worse, he didn't have a clue how she'd managed to get hold of his address.

He despatched the swear word-loaded rejection and hoped that maybe now the mental would leave him alone. Feeling distinctly better (to him insulting people was the equivalent of a nicotine rush, whilst being as addictive as crack) he switched off his phone to prevent a response and left the house. He pulled the door to with a deliberately loud bang (to annoy the neighbours and wake Elodie), skipped down the steps (he liked the elevated position the front door had over the street) and walked towards his selfishly-parked Hummer. Smiling again, he felt in his Dom Perignon-laden water that today was going to be a good day.

Elodie sat up in bed when she heard the front door slam. She rubbed her eyes, smearing some make-up in the process. She burned with anger; being French she had an overdeveloped sense of (she's) right and (they're) wrong. She'd heard Hershey's every uttered word, only feigning sleep.

As was her habit Elodie swore heavily under her breath. She hated Hershey treating her like this, like some common whore from the docks. But worse she hated herself for letting him get away with it. Hershey's position meant Elodie could clamber up the corporate ladder in exchange for the temporary exploitation of her vagina.

She went into the bathroom, turned the shower to its highest setting and stepped under the cascade, keen for the heat and force of the water to blow the fury away.

I'm Not Stalking You, Honest

If someone were to follow me to work each morning they would think I take a random route. Not so, Sherlock. My walk from the train station to the office is based entirely on a whim and I will explain why...

There was a time when I took the same, dull fucking route twice a day. I won't bore you (or me!) with the details. One day, I forget exactly which, I was dragging my heels and looking at nothing in particular when a fantastic arse hove unexpectedly into view. One moment there was dull, grey boredom, the next a spectacular vision! Even better the arse was attached to a pretty decent pair of legs. The one downer was I couldn't see her tits properly because she was on the other side of the road, so I decided I'd take a closer look. With the barest of glances I cut across the stationary traffic, watching out for the obligatory twats on two wheels that refuse to queue with everyone else. I increased the speed of my gait as the gap with the arse widened temporarily. It was a good shape, pushing out of trousers that looked sprayed on, with just enough firm wobble. Not the jellyfish jiggle like the recently relieved pregnants (you know, the ones who moan about still having puppy fat) and not the plastic doll rigidity of the size zero's either. I judged it a great arse, at least a 7, maybe even a 7.5.

Then it disappeared, replaced by a fat guy; no a *huge* guy. The arse rating on this one was at best a -12. I stopped abruptly and looked around to regain sight of the trim bottom, but I almost immediately received a firm shove in the back.

"What the *fuck* are you doing?" snapped some bespectacled wanker who'd bumped into me when I'd halted in my tracks. He fired off a glare as he pushed through me.

I ignored him, instead scanning left and right to find the arse again. I spotted it relatively quickly, receding fast down a side road, going in completely the wrong direction to my office. I had a choice between fat guy going in the right direction or sexy arse, with unidentified tits which really still needed a closer inspection, going in the wrong direction.

Frankly it was a piss-easy choice and as a result I was fifteen minutes late for work that day. I've never looked back. Now, with hindsight, maybe that was another mistake — not knowing who was behind me.

Destinations

Mr Lamb had followed Dedman for a distance, still puzzled by his aberrant activity. The meandering walk that seemed only vaguely to lead to the office was utterly ambiguous. Every day this week the route Dedman had traced had been different and Mr Lamb could not figure out the reason why. Dedman didn't seem to be meeting anyone and he was certain there weren't any drop-off or pick-up points either.

He knew without looking at his watch that his time with Dedman had to be temporarily suspended. So leaving Dedman to his mystifying wanderings, he turned around and walked briskly in the opposite direction for exactly one hundred and fifteen seconds to the pre-arranged rendezvous point. Five seconds later and at exactly the appointed time he was sitting on the rear seat of an idling black Jaguar saloon with private licence plates. As he was pulling the door shut the Jaguar breezed silently away from the kerb and slotted neatly into the early morning traffic. Mr Lamb permitted the regal, silver-haired man to carry on reading his newspaper and instead looked at the world outside passing silently by. He thought it amusing (although he refrained from smiling) that such a macho, male-dominated profession tolerated a publication printed on pink paper.

After a couple of minutes studying the FT the man neatly folded the broadsheet and placed it precisely central between them on the highly-polished leather upholstery. He then interlaced his fingers on his lap, turned slightly and gave his full and rather intense attention to Mister Lamb, who knew the look well enough.

After five minutes of one-way discourse the silver-haired man nodded sharply and rapped on the window dividing passenger from driver. Mr Lamb took this as his cue that the monologue was over. Within moments he was on the kerb. The Jaguar pulled away and was lost in the teeming traffic.

He looked around briefly to get his bearings, then headed for the nearest tube station. He gave himself two more days to find out what the hell was really going on.

Serena looked up from the piece of paper in her hand. This was the right place, she knew, because the address and business names matched the discrete plaque fixed to the right of an imposing black door which gleamed as brightly as the brass. She pushed the paper into her handbag and hesitated briefly. This was her last chance to pull out.

No, I am made of stronger stuff than this, she told herself. And besides, what she did today would lead to the ultimate thrill and that, in the end, was the point of it all. After a deep breath she straight-armed the door and entered a reception area that looked just like a very plush surgery, which is exactly what it was.

Jack, too, had reached his destination, but he needed no map as he'd been to (although not in) this building many times before. He stood outside and looked enviously upwards at the glass walls stretching up to finger the heavens. Behind each pane, he suspected, was a thrusting young executive forging his way in the dog-eat-dog world of business.

He brought his vision back down to earth, visibly squared his shoulders, pushed his chest out, marched up to the revolving doors and pushed hard at them. He stepped in, performed two 360° turns and ended up back where he started. He strode away from the building without looking back.

I should be in there with the bastards, he swore to himself, and one day I *will* be in there with them.

Just not today.

Hershey was in his white Hummer (if it's good enough for Arnie, it's good enough for Hershey, he'd decided), a bit of jazz on the radio. However the cheery melody wasn't lifting his spirits. The traffic was, to put it mildly, fucking awful. He was crawling along, bumper to bumper. Everything on two wheels or two feet was moving at a faster rate than him and buses were rattling along their private lanes with impunity. That the less affluent were reaching their destinations faster simply shredded his nerves. And on public fucking transport as well. It was times like these that made him glad he didn't pay tax to the UK government.

The next five minutes saw his Hummer nudge forward no more than a couple of car-lengths, whilst three buses and countless bikes and pedestrians undertook him, which was made even more annoying as Hershey was seated on the left side of the car. A few hundred yards in front he saw the lights change from red to green and back to red again. He was very aware of the time ticking away. As the queue of cars concertinaed he squeezed forward another painfully short distance.

Hershey had finally had enough. The lights turned red to amber.

"Fuck this," he grumbled.

He stamped on the accelerator and yanked on the steering wheel, putting the Hummer into the bus lane as the lights went green. The car spurted forward as fuel gushed into the greedy engine and he pressed his foot all the way to the floor in an effort to reach the lights before they changed back to red.

Too late, they flicked amber and then red. Hershey knew he had to get back into the legitimate lane as there was CCTV everywhere in this goddamned city. Quick as a flash he saw, and took, his chance, cutting in front of a Ford which was merely coasting in the queue and in no apparent hurry.

As he slid his Hummer into the gap the Ford driver woke up to the fact that he was being carved up, but his realisation came too late. Hershey grinned manically and the man raised his hands in frustration.

"Fuck you!" Hershey shouted. The Ford beeped his horn causing Hershey to give the guy the finger and say, "Jerk!"

Hershey could imagine the man simmering behind him. Although he'd absolutely no right to feel indignant, Hershey was pissed off at the guy and determined to get his own back. The lights changed again and Hershey rolled forward, but only at the pace of a mollusc. Just as he reached the lights they started to turn to amber again. Hershey held on until the last moment, as the red bulb was beginning to glow, then accelerated through leaving the Ford stranded.

As Ford guy flashed his lights in frustration Hershey waved cheerily in his rear view mirror, pleased he'd righted the wrong.

Claire started with surprise when she realised her boss was looming at her shoulder. Patricia Hodges (the 'P' of P&R PR) was a heavy-boned woman, her mass increased by the welter of gold and well-padded Chanel suits she wore as a method of displaying her wealth. However, those that spent time with Ms. Hodges soon learned by observation that she always wore the same jewellery and rotated three suits, proving her appearance was as shallow as her character.

Claire forced a grin before she swivelled round to face her boss. She stayed seated. Patricia liked to dominate her staff and Claire couldn't afford to lose her job.

"Morning Patricia!" Claire trilled in forced good humour.

"Would you like to join the lengthening queue of the great failures the government quaintly refers to as *job seekers*?" Patricia launched. She was always direct and never dealt in pleasantries.

"Um, no. I enjoy my job," Claire lied.

"Then in that case you need to generate some more business for the company. Your rolling monthly stats are slipping below the median measure."

P&R PR used a recurring revenue measurement method to track who was performing well and who wasn't. Those who generated below-average incomes for a period of three months were put on a warning then, if underperformance continued, were summarily sacked. Patricia thought this a clever way of driving continued growth as it meant her staff were forced to bring in more business to stay ahead, so driving up the average and dragging the laggards along with them. That this created less than savoury behaviour from some of her employees bothered Patricia not in the least. As long as it was legal, who cared?

"Well, were you aware that your performance is failing?" Patricia demanded.

"Of course," said Claire. Patricia's employees had to be on the ball, even if it was a different one.

"Then what are you doing about it?"

"I have a prospect I've been attempting to get a meeting with."

"Who?"

"Too early to reveal details," Claire said, knowing full well that Patricia would happily take the information to one of her star performers and she'd be out of a job in no time. It had happened before.

Patricia's face turned down even further, if that were possible. "You play it that way then, Claire. But you need to be aware you're on *very* thin ice. You need to get your bony backside out of that chair more often and into the field if you're to survive in *my* company."

"It's well in hand, Patricia."

"Good, it had better be. And it's Ms. Hodges to you."

Claire stuck out her tongue as her boss strode away.

So Where's Toto?

With a hefty wedge of misfortune I manage to enter my place of work on the hour because the girl I'd been following happens to go into a building adjacent to mine, so ultimately I'd meandered little.

At the time it never occurred to me that what I'm doing could be considered a diluted form of stalking by the average man on the street. I say diluted as I don't think I've ever followed the same girl twice. The only 'selection criterion' is the quality of the vision in front of me, otherwise there is no pattern, which sounds terrible now I read back what I've written down. I would have had a tough time explaining it to the cops too. I've never been in trouble with the law so I can only imagine their interrogation techniques, and Gene Hunt looms large in my mind...

"Now then *Mister* Dedman, would you care to explain *why* you follow gorgeous women every day?" asks Good Cop mildly.
"Erm, because they're gorgeous?" I reply without attempting a hint at irony.
"Stop *fucking* us around and just answer the *fucking* question you t-*wat!*" shouts Bad Cop and bangs his fist on the table, then in my face.
And so on...

The Bank's busty, fifty-something receptionist (arse score of 5) wakes me from my imaginings, cooing a "Hello!" at me as I stride across the marble floor towards the lift. I think she has a mothering thing for me. I wave back and thank the Gods of the Almighty Dollar/Sterling/Yuan/Euro (delete as applicable) that the lift door is yawning wide and so I can step straight into the steel box dangling precariously in mid-air on spindly cables (I don't like lifts) and press the button for my floor. The lift hasn't started up yet so I press the button again, several times until the doors close and the box lurches upwards. I shiver.

The load on the soles of my feet increases as the lift blasts through the floors then I feel briefly lighter as it decelerates past twelve and thirteen before stopping at fourteen. The doors open and I step out into a cool open-plan office that has been buzzing with life for hours already, occupied for long stretches of the day tracking the various indices — Asia, Europe and finally the Americas, as the activity of making money chases the sun across the time zones.

Fortunately I'm not stuck in the open plan; I get an office all to myself. Okay, it hasn't the greatest of views (into another business the opposite side of the road where a couple of fat blokes reside) but at least I can shut the door and block the noise out if I feel antisocial. I nod at a few acquaintances as I thread between the desks. Because I always head back home as soon as the nine-to-five ends I don't have any real friends at work. There's no partying for sad old Josh. I've found that maintaining even an association requires constant effort, like tending a garden. But anyway, who wants to be friends with a banker?

These days I make bloody sure nobody knows what I used to do. There's a joke I know that just about says it all:

One day in class the teacher is asking the children what their parents are employed as.
"Policeman," says one kid. "Nurse," says another. Each one answers in turn except for little Johnny. The teacher is very surprised as he is normally the first to speak.
Eventually she says, "Johnny, what does your father do?"
Johnny looks furtive and refuses to answer.
The teacher presses him.
"Well okay," Johnny sighs. "My dad works in a club as a male prostitute and lets men bang his arse for money all night long."
The teacher is lost for words. She cannot believe her ears. When she dismisses the class she keeps Johnny back.
"Johnny, is that true about your father?"
"No miss. He's a banker really, but I was too embarrassed to say."

I drop my man-bag on the floor, flick on the computer and whilst it's booting up check out the view from my window. Only one fat bloke is in the opposite office. I wave at him but he just stares, then turns his back on me. Unless he has eyes in the back of his head he can't see the finger I give the rude bastard.

"Knock, knock!" Liam pokes his head in. "Brought you a coffee."

"Coffee's always welcome, come in, mate," I say, hoping he didn't see my less than social gesture reflected in the window.

Liam passes me a cup. Not some crappy Starbucks stuff, but from an interestingly named specialist place that had recently opened nearby and that I'd never heard of until Liam discovered it. I take the plastic lid off the paper cup and sniff the roasted aroma assaulting my nostrils. I *love* coffee and I have a compatriot in Liam who seems to adore the bean even more than me. He's probably the only person in the Bank I have any time for. We'd just started talking a week ago and before I knew it Liam was popping in regularly to visit.

"You made it on time today, then?" Liam flickers a smile.

"Train was on schedule for once," I reply, which strictly is entirely true.

"I don't know how you do that journey twice a day."

I shrug. "It's not too bad once you get used to it."

"The best thing for your career would be a move into London."

I'm sure you can tell by now that Liam works in Human Resources, but unlike every other HR person I've ever met he's reasonable and seems proficient. But it's early days and probably too soon for his colleagues to bugger up his abilities.

I genuinely like Liam, primarily because he doesn't seem to give a shit about money, his money at least. Most people employed by banks care far too much about the contents of their own handmade leather wallets and not enough about those of their clients. Fucking vampires the lot of them — they only survive off someone else's misery. Sometimes I imagine staking everyone in the office with a sharpened biro. A red one.

I shake my head. "I tried it for a few months but I didn't like it and shifted back home. But the girlfriend keeps a flat here."

"She wears the trousers then?" Liam laughs.

I choke out a laugh. "Course not!"

Liam smiles as he takes a sip of his coffee. He's an older guy, dresses very well and very neatly but I don't know a great deal about him yet. I'm about to ask him a question about his life outside work but the phone steals my thunder.

"Bollocks," I say, recognising the number. I let it ring.

Liam walks round the desk. He's familiar with the caller too.

"You're not going to answer that, are you," Liam states. He's already well aware of the antipathy I have towards Hershey because I'm one of those people who wear their bleeding heart on their sleeves.

"No fucking way."

"He'll know you're in, he'll have checked with his sources," Liam advises.

I know Liam is right. "I could be off having a shit," I argue. The phone stops ringing and I gloat. "Told you he'd go away."

An instant message pings up on my computer. I wiggle the mouse to bring the screen alive. It says, "I know you're in your office. Come and see me. Now. H."

"Ah bugger," I say, ignoring Liam's microscopic smile of success.

"What's the problem between you two?" Liam asks.

I shrug. "Oz can fucking wait. I haven't finished my coffee yet."

"Oz?" Liam frowns.

"As in 'Wizard Of...'"

Liam shakes his head.

"You've seen the film, right?" I ask. Liam nods. "There's the bit near the end where the Wizard's big face is on the screen and Toto finds an old guy making it all up. Well, don't look behind the curtain because you'll be disappointed."

The penny drops and Liam says, "Ah." He doesn't look particularly taken by my lateral attempt at humour. No move into stand-up comedy for me then.

"Look, I need to go," I say. "Thanks for the coffee."

"Good, best not to keep Hershey waiting for long, otherwise he'll be putting another complaint into HR about you."

"Nope, I'm off to the bog 'cos I actually am in serious need of a shit."

Liam shakes his head in mock dismay as I depart. I head in the direction of the middle managers' bathroom, which thankfully isn't far away. I'm barely six feet into the open plan when my phone starts ringing insistently again. Bizarrely I do desperately need a crap and I prefer to avoid a burst bowel to seeing Hershey Fucking Valentine's smug chops. I enter the toilet stall at the far end of the toilet block, pull my trousers down and settle to some serious sanitary business.

Exterminate!

Hershey Valentine fumed as he slammed the phone back into its cradle. He knew full well that Dedman was taking the piss out of him. He screwed his face up into a ball as he imagined the despicable little bastard laughing along with all his little low-lifes in the office. Hershey absolutely couldn't stand to have his authority being challenged, no siree, no fucking way. The trouble was he couldn't and wouldn't court direct confrontation with his victims, particularly in front of others, not unless he was 100% solid with his evidence. Then he revelled in being judge, jury and exe-fucking-cutioner and would rip the offender to pieces. Hershey wished he'd been born 200 years ago. He could envisage himself as a hanging judge (although he couldn't imagine swapping his Hummer for a horse and his cell for parchment).

So Hershey found himself caught momentarily between a rock and a hard place — outright insubordination by a reportee on the one hand, but a plum opportunity for personal embarrassment if he got it wrong. It wasn't a particularly cheery combination.

However, his need for absolute authority and the expectation of compliance quickly won the brief mental tug of war. He decided to go and face down the imp. He jumped up from his chair, energised by a burst of indignant adrenalin, then stalked down the corridor of power that existed on the penultimate floor of the Bank and so to the lift. He tapped his foot as he waited impatiently for the doors to open. The adrenalin dipped as he did so and he almost returned to his office, but just as he was almost overwhelmed by doubt a cheerful ping announced the lift's arrival. Hershey stepped in to the metal box. His stomach lurched briefly as the lift dropped three floors.

He stepped out into the open-plan office; his irritation peaked again when he saw that no one paid any attention to his entry. He marched through the space stalking like a parrot, all stiff and erect.

Fuck you, he thought. No favours will ever be bestowed on you lot.

Josh's door yawned open. He walked in but the office was as empty as a sigh. He swung around and went to the nearest desk. A non-descript guy was blabbering on the phone. Hershey poked out a finger and disconnected the call.

"Hey!" the guy started to protest, but then he saw who it was. "Oh, what's the matter Mr Valentine?"

"Dedman, where is he?" Hershey demanded.

The guy thought for a moment, blank-faced. He shrugged. "I'm not sure," he said.

"Idiot," Hershey replied, and the guy's face darkened perceptibly.

"He went in the direction of the toilet," someone said, another vacant face.

Hershey parroted off across the office without thanking his informant. He entered the gents and paused momentarily. There was no one at the urinals and all the stall doors appeared closed. As his heels rang on the floor Hershey looked in one stall after another until he stood at the last one. A quick push and he knew it was occupied.

Hershey did his piranha impression, all teeth, no smile.

Bombs Away!

After a couple of minutes straining I hear the toilet door open and the click of heels on the lino floor. I listen as the first stall door is pushed back on its hinges. Click, click, click. Another door opens. This process is repeated until the heels stand outside my door.

"I know you're in there Dedman," he says in a sleazy American drawl.

"Look Hershey, I'm having a shit," I reply. "Can I have some peace, please." At that moment my bowel chooses to release a large quantity of gas accompanied by a sound that sounds like my arse is being torn in half. If I could high five my digestive system I'd do it right here and now.

"I'll be waiting for you in your office," Hershey says when the fart echo dies. The heels retreat out of the toilet block.

I take another couple of minutes to finish up (I'm in no hurry), flush, step out of the stall and wash my hands. I stare at myself in the mirror. I'm already looking stressed and knackered and it's not even 9.30am.

Then a thought occurs to me and I return to the stall. I piss briefly on my hand (there's not a lot of fluid left after all that activity) and shake the excess off so I'm damp but not dripping. I leave the toilet, forcing down the urge to wash my soiled hand, to face Hershey.

Who's That Girl?

Hershey looked around and took a momentary personal satisfaction from the austere decorative style imposed upon Josh's office space. He sat in the visitor's chair, then stood up again. He wasn't sure where best to position himself. He decided on Josh's backside residence, flopped down and put his feet up on the desk. The seat was lumpy and uncomfortable. He hoped it gave Dedman piles. His eye was caught by a photograph on Josh's desk which caused him to return his feet to earth, lean over, stretch out an arm and pick up the frame to take a closer look.

What an ugly bitch, he thought. *No, not ugly*, he corrected himself. *Plain, very, very plain.What a perfect match for someone in a mundane role*, Hershey mused.

Therefore Josh's choice was ultimately no surprise when he thought about it. On the other hand Hershey reluctantly admitted that Josh certainly could, from a looks perspective, do much better, which simply confirmed his view of the world. Looks weren't everything, money was. It was a fundamental fact deserved of Newton or Einstein. But of course, neither was as clever as Hershey.

He liked his girls blonde, rather than mousy brown like this one. He was able to use those strongest of aphrodisiacs — money and power — to draw in surprisingly attractive girls for, despite his thoughts otherwise, Hershey was not particularly good-looking himself. He was tall and wiry. His well-tanned face (from a multitude of skiing holidays) was unlined but only because of regular Botox applications. He had a forehead that was frankly too high and a haircut that was so flat it must have been squared off with a spirit level. Hershey's favourite celeb was Simon Cowell, appreciating his arrogance and utter self-belief.

The girl looked familiar, but Hershey couldn't entirely place the face. He tapped the frame on his chin as he thought, momentarily forgetting the lie he was about to deliver to Dedman.

It's All Yours

My shit had been one of those extremely satisfying ones where, during the smooth delivery of the brown log and for a few moments subsequently, a satisfying glow courses through me. Like love but without the complications, although some clearing-up is also needed afterwards. As a result the dump hormones are still pinging around in my bloodstream so I don't perceive the presence of my beloved boss at my desk — *my desk,* with his feet up, reclining in *my* chair — until I am well inside my office. Finding someone sitting uninvited in your office isn't a comfortable sight to my mind, it's a territorial thing. But far, far worse is to find an interloper actually sitting where you toil. Ask any man and he'll tell you so. A junior visitor means someone is after your job but can't do anything about it, a senior visitor means someone is *really* after your job and can do everything about it.

What's bizarre is I'm far more irritated by Hershey's location than him holding my girlfriend in the grip of his slimy palm. I should have known then that something was wrong with our relationship.

At first Hershey doesn't notice me; apparently he's lost in thought, or more likely he's asleep with his eyes open. A number of ideas occur to me — backing out and going to the toilet again, or shouting 'Oi, wanker!' This one appeals, as it would be funny to see whether I could get him to tumble out of my chair and maybe break an arm. Or his neck. Thinking of necks makes me then consider sneaking up behind Hershey and strangling the bastard. But my indecision is my hangman's noose and before I can decide between fight or flight something cracks Hershey's reverie. He looks up and stares at me as if he's never met me before, as if we've never talked whilst I break wind.

"Hershey, hi," I say, uncertainty and irritation smothering my voice in equal concentrations.

"Uh, Josh," Hershey replies in his grating twang. So he does know me after all.

My pointed look is intended to show my displeasure with him sitting at my desk, but it's a mistake as he just smiles and leans back in my seat to further impose himself.

"I tried to call you earlier," he tells me.

"Oh, I didn't know," I reply with an unapologetic and utterly insincere shrug. "I've hardly been in my office all morning for reasons you're aware of." An ailing look passes over Hershey's face but I don't give a shit (even though I just have).

"Who's this?" Hershey nutmegs me with his sudden change of subject. He waves Claire's picture around, one taken in happier times.

"Not that it's any of your business," I say, deliberately pissy in an attempt to restore my teetering balance, "but it's my girlfriend. Why?"

"It's just she looks familiar. What's her name?"

"Claire."

A hint of something like recognition flitters through the synapses that must loiter behind Hershey's eyes (one thing he's not is stupid). "Claire Pigeon? Works for P&R PR?"

"Yes, that's her," I try to hide my astonishment and fail utterly, which brings another awful grin to Hershey's teeth. "How did you know?"

Hershey shrugged. "Knowledge is power," he says, grin still fixed.

What a twat, I think. Do normal people really make those sorts of comments?

But then I don't consider Hershey to be a human, he's more of a bacteria or a viral infection in a body suit. He looks at Claire's picture one more time, then places the frame face down on the desk as if then she can't intrude on our conversation. He drops his feet off the desk, spins the chair ninety degrees so that he is able to plant his forearms on the glass surface before he hunches his shoulders in a show of gravitas he doesn't possess.

"Josh. Josh my friend. I need your help," he says. Yet another unexpected statement. It's clearly his day for revelations. With a sweeping arm he generously indicates that I should sit in the guest's chair. Clearly Hershey forgets that he is the interloper, not I. However in my curiosity I fail to argue and drop into the seat, giving me a view of my office that I've never had before, like sitting in the rear of your car.

"Help with what, Hershey?" Damn my inquisitiveness!

"Do you recall that presentation I've been writing to give at the Exchange?" Hershey asks.

I certainly do, because it's my fucking presentation, not his. I've done all the heavy lifting to put it together, Hershey simply adding a couple of perfumed phrases. He's the dog that the flea of creativity rarely bites.

He continues whilst I simmer. "Well I won't be able to deliver it and Mr Culpepper would like you," he points finger and thumb at me like a gun, then drops the hammer, "to take my place."

My heart soars, momentarily ignoring what might be behind the hat-trick of stunners my odious superior has just delivered. I've put hours into that presentation and it's a prestigious event, lots of industry movers and shakers will be there. Then my head catches up with my sprinting heart because, like any good banker, Hershey will ensure there will be some sort of cost associated with the deal, heavily weighted in his favour, which only a monumental effort will pay off.

"Thanks Hershey," I start saying, but he interrupts and bats my words away like flies as if the effort is nothing to him.

"Really, it's nothing. I'm having lunch with the Old Men," he says. For 'Old Men' read 'Ian Culpepper', the Bank's chairman, and Sir David Cowan, the giver and taker of careers. It's an effortless trade for a crappy presentation to a few anonymous suits.

I hardly hear Hershey over the roar of blood in my eardrums. "Sorry?" I mumble.

"I said the presentation is at 10am." He checks his watch. "Better shake your tail feathers if you're going to make it in time."

And at that he levers himself up from my desk and nonchalantly strolls out of my office with a wink. I watch my chair spin around a few times before it comes to rest as if Hershey was never here.

I remember then that I have piss on my hands.

Orgasm Addict

Serena wasn't usually self-conscious when it came to sitting around with her vagina on view for everyone to see, but there was something intangible about this clinic that unnerved her. No one was being judgemental, in fact it was just the opposite as the nurse and doctor were thoroughly scrupulous in their attitude towards her. She couldn't quite put her finger on it and the feeling niggled away.

So far she had been subjected to an internal swab and the extraction of a vial full of blood from a troublesome vein. She'd been told the results wouldn't be available straight away. Even in this era it still took time for an analysis to be carried out, a letter to be typed, printed and posted. The clinic promised to be fast, but it would be days before the assessment dropped through her letterbox and Serena would know whether she was free of sexually-transmitted diseases or not.

It was (literally) a hard fact that Serena had shagged a large number of men. The vast majority of her partners had refused to wear condoms and she hadn't argued with them because she didn't like the horrible insensitive things either (or the condoms). However, she wasn't worried. It's not that she didn't care; she simply knew her mind would report on any viral incursions. Besides her intellectual belief, there were no physical telltale signs such as an itch or inflammation and all in all she felt entirely healthy.

However, the adult sex film industry (as it quaintly called itself) had become self-regulating of late. As always seemed to be the way, the problem had first arisen in the United States where an HIV-infected performer had temporarily shut down the lucrative business — the impact on earning potential meant testing and certification of performers became an absolute. No test and no pass meant no work, unless you were prepared to partake in under-the-counter productions which had their own risks. Typically they attracted the really sleazy actors and she absolutely didn't need to shag that type. There were plenty of bars in Margate where she could pick up far rougher men that had proper drug habits.

The nurse waited for her as she dressed behind a gauze screen. Once fully-clothed she led her through to see Dr

Hasp, the only noise the efficient-sounding rap of the nurse's heels on the tiled floor. When she entered the doctor's office Serena saw the rear of a wiry, grey-haired man seated at a desk, writing. As she stood uncertainly in the doorway she cast an appraising eye around the rest of the room. Unlike every other practitioner's surgery she had been into the office was conspicuously tidy. There was no pile of patient records, no tumble of medical magazines, no box of kids' toys — Serena couldn't imagine a parent bringing a child somewhere like this.

"Sit down would you, please, Miss, er, Serena." Hasp indicated an empty leather seat ninety degrees to the desk, his back still to her. Serena blushed slightly at the obvious disbelief the doctor showed in her alias.

He must see loads like me, she thought. Every single day, liar after liar after liar.

Serena sat as bidden and demurely crossed her legs. She reclined slightly, forcing herself to look more relaxed than she actually felt, trying to crush the blush. Finally Hasp shuffled the papers into a neat pile, capped his Cross fountain pen then slipped it into his shirt pocket. He twisted in his chair and took her in with an emotionless expression.

"It's just Serena, Doctor."

"How are you feeling Serena?" Hasp asked a second later, steepling his fingers as he awaited her reply.

She paused, momentarily held by Hasp's eyes, which were wide and unblinking, intense, deep pools which seemed to draw her in, suck her dry. They were bad fucking news. People with secrets didn't like to be analysed and Serena had plenty she wanted to keep private. She wondered whether the Hippocratic oath extended to sex doctors.

"Fine," she eventually lied.

"Good, good." Hasp removed the pen from his shirt pocket and tapped it on the paper atop his OCD-clean desk. "You filled in a questionnaire when you first arrived."

Serena nodded. She remembered the long list of questions like:

Has sex become the most important thing in your life? *Yes.*
Do you often find yourself preoccupied with sexual thoughts? *Yes.*
Do you ever feel bad about your sexual behaviour? *Yes.*
Have you attempted to stop some parts of your sexual behaviour? *No!!!*

Has anyone in your family ever been hurt by your sexual behaviour? *No (James was away too much to be aware of what was going on...I think).*

Do you ever think of your sexual behaviour being stronger than you are? *Yes (thankfully).*

And so on, for about fifty questions of an increasingly destructive nature, signifying behaviour on cruising, dogging and prostitution. She found it a little scary. Was this the path she was doomed to follow? She told herself not. But she also knew that addicts were good at kidding themselves, then kidded herself she was nothing of the sort.

"Do you consider yourself an addict, Serena?" Hasp said, taking off his wire-rimmed glasses and putting them on the desk.

"I can't go a day without coffee," she joked. Hasp smiled thinly.

"This is what we call the *Sexual Addiction Screening Test*," Hasp said, like it was an everyday thing.

"Oh." Serena inexplicably felt a weight drop inside. All her repressed feelings of guilt and shame from the dubious encounter with Handsome Guy on the train geysered up to the surface again and she felt herself blush anew.

"We use *SAST* to help in the assessment of sexually compulsive behaviour," Hasp said. He seemed to favour drip-feeding little titbits of information, like they were hard-to-digest lumps of factual gristle.

Serena shifted in her seat. "I'm not sure I understand."

"That's often the trouble," Hasp replied with a slight tilt of his head. "A high *SAST* score is a leading indicator of being a sexual addict."

"Wow." Serena decided she preferred it when Hasp was being obtuse but now the genie was out of the bottle her head swirled with the implications.

The doctor passed over her score sheet. Serena's hand shook slightly as she took the pages filled with narrow point text. Right at the top was a chart, the single bar stretched well into the red, which Serena assumed wasn't good. She rated a 9.0 on the sexual Richter scale, a destructive force to say the least. She flipped through the pages until she reached the last one. It appeared to be a certificate with her name in large, bold characters and underneath the pronunciation:

ADDICT

It felt like a penal (rather than penile) sentence and she shuddered with the implication. She thought she could hear Hasp talking again so she forced herself back to the surface of her consciousness.

Hasp was saying, "...of course this doesn't mean you are *categorically* a sex addict."

Ha! Serena laughed to herself.

"I would like to make a further appointment with you. We have an additional, deeper assessment called *SARA*, the Sexual Addiction Risk Assessment, which we can undertake."

"And how will this help me?" Serena was beginning to feel a little bruised with the doctor's relentless onslaught.

"It's a personal profile. It identifies your type of addiction and the risks you might be running. From this we can develop a plan of treatment," Hasp said, handing over his business card. "Give me a call to set something up. But I must warn you, it isn't a cheap process. I would need to see you on several occasions."

Money. Everything was always down to fucking *money*. Serena hardened immediately. She stood quickly.

"May I keep this?" She waved the paper around. She was a bomb primed and ready to go off.

"Of course." Hasp looked a little taken aback by her sudden shift in demeanour. "It is your analysis after all and with information we become empowered towards change."

What crap, Serena thought but instead she said, "Good. I'll see myself out."

Hasp's mouth dropped open, but before he could verbalise Serena walked out of the office, swept through reception, past sex fiends waiting patiently to be patronised by Hasp, and outside.

She turned her face to the sun, upset it wasn't raining. She felt dirtier than ever and didn't have a clue how to rinse the sensation away.

Jack watched the joggers trot past him. He hated them, the sight of all that wobbling fat made him feel nauseous. He thought they should keep all that blubber hidden away. Or eat less. Or die.

He looked at his watch, made a big show of it. A senior executive at lunch, that was him. Albeit an early lunch. Did that make it brunch? He didn't know. It was a stupid bloody word anyway. But it was irrelevant because he was waiting for his *client* (Jack liked that word!).

He picked up the Financial Times. Jack must have tried to read it twenty times at least. Most of it didn't make the slightest bit of sense, it was gobbledygook. Futures, options, what were they? He didn't have a clue.

His things were computers and software; now he really understood how they ticked.

"About time," Jack mumbled to himself as his client strolled into sight. He stood up, waiting to greet him on a level footing because that was what his management books advised he should do.

Death Warmed Up

I've made it. As I catch my breath a plush lift sweeps me upwards through a rather grand old building. Standing next to me is a besuited porter in a natty uniform replete with a top hat. It's like being in a 1930s hotel and I wonder if I'll be expected to tip the guy.

Before I can decide the lift glides to a halt, the doors part and the porter bows slightly. He exits a step ahead of me and leads me along a corridor carpeted in a luxurious, deep pile and through some heavy wooden double doors. A moment later and I'm at the front of an auditorium whose seats are full of cloned suits arranged in horseshoe-shaped rows. They seem to go on forever, up into eaves so high there are probably pigeons with vertigo hunkered down in the shadows.

Bloody hell, I think.

Suddenly I'm somewhat daunted by the prospect of presenting to all this lot. I'd assumed it was going to be some cosy affair, a few people arranged casually around a table and a projection screen. Normally standing up in front of a crowd doesn't faze me, but this was going to be like teaching in a classroom the size of the O_2 arena — lots of fucking effort for minimal return and terrifying in the process.

Then the sickest man I've ever seen still upright and breathing shuffles over to interrupt my dread thoughts and pumps my hand with more vigour than he really should. I worry he'll have a heart attack with the effort. He literally looks the personification of death warmed up; a pasty, lined face inset with dead eyes on a neck so scrawny it would embarrass a vulture, and capped with white hair. His emaciated body is clad in a suit that would have been expensive two decades ago. Bluntly, he looks fucking awful.

"Thank you for coming," he croaks, sounding like a toad speaking from inside the corpse of a crow. "We're delighted, really *delighted* to have you here after all. We were ever so upset when you cancelled yesterday."

Cancelled? I think. *Yesterday?* But my brain is too addled, too off-balance with the abrupt turn of events and a modicum of dread to pay full attention.

The effort all seems too much and the near-deceased breaks into a hacking cough. The room darkens slightly. It takes him a few moments to regain his breath and the gloom lifts as if Thanatos (Death himself to you and I) has reluctantly receded without a victim. He bangs his chest hard with his fist, presumably giving himself CPR. The mostly-departed has the strength to press a remote control into my hands.

"For the projector," he says.

"Thanks," I mumble in reply.

"Right, we'd better introduce you," he croaks, a flicker of the eyebrows as if to say, *Let's get this show on the road.*

The crusty old guy turns to face the audience. As I wonder where he's parked his ventilator my eyes mooch over the faceless men and women in suits and I only pay scant attention to what is being said.

"Ladies and gentlemen," he grates, "Thank you for waiting for a few minutes, I am sure you'll find the delay well worth it! We have here with us today a speaker of great note, a man with many years' experience in the money market. Without further embellishment, for none is needed, may I introduce Mr Hershey Valentine to give an outline on fiscal measures for the 21st Century."

What the fuck? Did I hear that right? I think to myself. *Hershey?*

"Erm, excuse me," I say and I tug on the corpse's sleeve as I try to check his departure (and his pulse).

"Is everything all right?" asks the cadaver. His rheumy eyes are everywhere but on me, probably looking for his oxygen mask.

"Cool," I say.

"Good." Hack, hack, then he starts shuffling away again.

I trot after the slothful stiff and catch him by a bony arm. I swear he is cold to the touch.

"Mr Valentine, what seems to be the matter, hmm?" The tone of his question is heavy and weary.

Then lightning strikes me, my mind fizzes with the possibilities. If they think I am Valentine then I can have some serious fun at his expense!

"Well, Mr Valentine?"

"Erm, it's rather a delicate matter," I say and lean in to him. "You see I have a...umm...disability."

"Oh dear! I hope it's nothing too debilitating?" He pulls back as if I have a virulent disease, then realises what he's done, attempts to rectify his politically incorrect attitude by putting a concerned look on his face, but fails miserably. Even though I'm not disabled I'm less than impressed by his behaviour.

"Not physically, no." I play it dumb.

"Good! Well it's very pleasing that your Bank employs someone with a disability. It is to be commended." Then the old bastard walks off. I shrug mentally. He can't say I didn't try to warn him.

As the lights dim the limited chatter dwindles away entirely and the title of my presentation appears on the screen.

"Fiscal measures for the 21st century," I say. "Fuck!"

The crowd looks at me in awe or shock, I can't decide which. For the first time I wonder whether I've made a mistake. Then it goes from bad to worse. Within ten minutes the assembly dissolves into complete and utter farcical chaos. This is how:

Two minutes — a handful of people get up and leave the auditorium in disgust.
Five minutes — the audience has halved.
Eight minutes — Mr Cadaver returns to the room.
He watches my performance in open-mouthed shock. The auditorium is almost empty.
Eight minutes and thirty seconds — The Mummy tries to tug me off the floor but I bridle,
still irritated by his less than generous attitude to the disabled (which I temporarily am).
Nine minutes — I shrug him off which is easy, he has the strength of a sparrow.
Nine minutes and thirty seconds — the projector dies,
Skeleton Boy wiggles the remote control at me in triumph. There are three people left in the audience.
Ten minutes — he shuffles across the floor and rants at me. Someone claps at the back.

"*Mister* Valentine! Whatever has got into you?" demands The Dead Man Shambling.

"Got into me? I don't understand what you, fuck!, mean! Here I am giving a perfectly rational, wanker!, presentation when people, cunt!, start having a go at me and leaving. Fuck! What's the problem?"

"The *problem* is precisely *that*," he says and points an unsteady digit at my mouth. I can't tell if the instability in his limb is infirmity or fury, not that I care either way.

"What?" I intelligently play dumb.

"Your diction, sir, is the problem."

"Oh," I say, as if I finally get it, "You mean, bollocks!, my disability."

"Disability?" The goldfish has clearly forgotten our previous discussion. "What do you mean, *disability*?"

"Yes, disability, twat!, Tourette's."

The dead guy looks really confused now. "Tourette's?"

"Uh-huh. Uncontrolled, fuck!, swearing."

The corpse slaps his forehead. "Holy shit!"

"My point exactly. Bollocks."

"I'll be speaking to your Chairman. I think you need to leave now."

"And I think you're being prejudiced. Tourette's is a legitimate, fuck!, medical condition."

"Leave. Now."

I do.

An Espresso or Two

Mr Lamb sat in a small cafe waiting for his employer to arrive. The place was upmarket and well off the beaten track, a combination, whether by luck or design, that would ensure the cafe was either a sure-fire hit or an abject failure. Sadly, from the lack of clientele, it looked like the latter would be the most likely outcome. However the cafe's loss was Mr Lamb's gain. He liked the anonymity of the place. No customers meant no eavesdropping and they made pretty good coffee, which was an essential part of life, he felt.

He had to smile to himself again as he cast his mind backwards. He'd sat in the back row of the auditorium, so far from Josh his face was only a smudge in the distance. Mr Lamb, who had made it his business of late to get under the skin of Mr Dedman and several of his colleagues, had to admit the performance had come at him from the blindside, like being taken out by a zealous defender in a two-footed, bone-crunching sliding tackle. Here was a relatively senior representative of the Bank, an erudite and frankly dull character, standing in front of a prestigious audience and...swearing. The profanities had tumbled out in an increasing torrent from Dedman's mouth as he gained in apparent confidence. Initially the audience had reacted with disbelief, then disgust and then revulsion. Within minutes the listeners had stopped listening and were streaming away.

But no one attempted to stop Dedman until the ancient man from another millennium had remonstrated with him and then had him thrown out. Mr Lamb quite enjoyed seeing the pompous suits in such an unfamiliar position and he made a mental note that perhaps Dedman wasn't quite as predictable as he'd assumed. However Mr Lamb knew Culpepper wouldn't be quite so appreciative of the discovery and would instead be more concerned with the Bank's image.

The cafe door burst open, shattering his thought process. He quickly adopted a poker face as a dapper, well dressed, tall, silver-haired man with the emotional presence of three people entered the cafe. After only a second's pause the man located Mr Lamb, which wasn't difficult as between them they were the only people in the cafe not adorned with an apron.

"Nice place," said Ian Culpepper, not really meaning it. He pulled out a chair and sat down. The Chairman didn't remove his jacket, a sure sign this would be a typically brief rendezvous.

"Excellent coffee too," Mr Lamb said. He knew the Bank's Chairman was a snob when it came to caffeine. It was one of the few things they had in common.

A waitress appeared at Culpepper's elbow, pad and pen at the ready, which Mr Lamb thought somewhat optimistic.

"Double espresso," Culpepper demanded without looking up. Mr Lamb shook his head at the questioning look from the waitress. His Americano (with an extra shot) was only half finished. She withdrew, her pad unsullied. A moment later a hissing sound erupted from the rear of the cafe as the staff gratefully busied themselves over the very shiny, expensive Italian import.

"I haven't got long," said Culpepper, glancing at his heavy gold watch to emphasise his statement.

"I won't take up much of your time," Mr Lamb assured him. He paused as the waitress delivered the espresso. Culpepper downed the powerful liquid in one and placed the diminutive cup back on the saucer none too gently.

"You're right, it is good coffee." Culpepper waved to get the waitress's attention then pointed at the cup for a refill

As the hissing sound filled the cafe again Culpepper focused his attention on Lamb and spread his hands wide to say, *So?* Although the Chairman habitually forced supplicants to wait for him (a simple but highly effective demonstration of power) he couldn't tolerate this behaviour in others for precisely the same reason. Immediately a small part of Mr Lamb's psyche took over and delivered the monologue on Dedman's performance. But at the same time the larger element of his intellect watched with amusement over his shoulder as Culpepper's expression grew gradually stonier. The espresso that had been deposited by the waitress only one sentence in sat untouched and rapidly cooling. When he'd finished speaking Mr Lamb sipped his coffee whilst Culpepper calmed down.

"Has this clarified your thinking?" Culpepper asked, his voice tight.

"I confess to still being…unclear. In fact now even more so. Dedman is displaying plenty of unusual behaviour, but no sign of anything criminal in nature. The others have also proven scrupulously clean so far."

Culpepper barked out a short, humourless noise that sounded more cough than laugh. He liked facts, data, numbers, calculations. He lived in a world where everything was either black or white. When any situation was grey he brought Mr Lamb in, but it also meant he had to devolve a degree of power to the other man and he didn't like it, not one bit. He felt the overwhelming urge to reassert himself. "A month ago £20 million was siphoned off from *my* Bank and today you still don't know who the culprit is," he stated.

"That is correct," Mr Lamb nodded.

Culpepper shook his head. "Fucking poor, Lamb. By your usual standard, very fucking poor."

Mr Lamb did not reply, did not respond in any visible way.

"I have considered the fact that this could be deliberate," Mister Lamb said, voicing a notion that had been bouncing around his brain cavity for some time.

"How so?"

"Perhaps Dedman is attempting to get himself fired?"

"Personally, after stealing a small fortune I'd be keeping my head down rather than drawing attention to myself."

"Maybe it is a double bluff."

"For fuck's sake I can't be doing with all this psychological crap." Culpepper sat back in his chair. "What do you suggest?"

Mr Lamb had considered that extensively and had an answer ready. "Continue to keep Dedman close at hand. Away from the office it would be much harder to keep a focus on him."

Culpepper wasn't happy but deferred to the suggestion. "Whatever happens, once this is over he's fucked nevertheless. Anyway, I can take it out on Valentine instead," Culpepper smirked. Then he stood and stalked out without a goodbye. A moment later the waitress was beside Mr Lamb.

"Can I get you anything else?" she asked, eyeing Culpepper's untouched cup with barely disguised distress — no pleasure had been obtained from the coffee beans which had been sacrificed for nothing.

"No thank you, just the bill please."

Mr Lamb didn't mind settling up. He probably wouldn't even put it on expenses. It wasn't a question of whether Culpepper would pay, simply that Mr Lamb had more money than he knew what to do with. Nothing and no one to spend it on, that was the problem.

Culpepper slid into his Jaguar, parked illegally directly outside the cafe. He hadn't got a ticket, but even if he had it wouldn't have been a problem as he knew the highest law in London. He had driven himself over as he'd no wish for his driver to see Mr Lamb a second time in one day. He clasped a palm over his sweating forehead, which pounded with the pressure of a thousand problems, any one of which could bring him down. Yet again he thought back to that shocking night a month ago, back to when this turmoil had all begun...

He had been at his desk poring over a set of accounts with his Financial Director, Edward Shoe, hovering by his side. It was Shoe, the bastard, who'd alerted him to the irregularity and, although he knew that ultimately there was no one that he could trust other than himself, at least Shoe could be scared sufficiently to keep his mouth shut. Culpepper knew far too much about him.

"I can't fucking see what you're on about," he said.

"There," Shoe replied in his perfect Queen's English and pointed to the screen. "It's actually very easy to spot."

"So why the fuck didn't we catch it sooner?" Culpepper growled. He tugged open a desk drawer, noisily popped out a couple of pain killers from a packet and downed them with a slug of single malt.

"Because we had to know specifically what to look out for and where. The year-end accounts had been signed off and closed so there was no reason to hunt for any irregularities. It was really rather clever of him. We shouldn't have found it."

Culpepper glared at the FD, not liking the appreciative tone in his voice. 'Clever' was not the word he'd have chosen.

"If you're expecting me to congratulate you you'll have a fucking long wait," he said. Shoe pursed his lips. He didn't like the Chairman swearing.

Culpepper steepled his fingers and thought for a moment. Shoe stayed quiet, knowing too well it would be unwise to intrude. Culpepper reached over to a pad sitting atop his desk and pulled it towards him. He picked up his pen and began to write.

"Transfer the money from this account to plug the hole," he ordered. He tore off a sheet of paper and handed it to Shoe. "And do everything to fucking hide the transaction."

"Are you sure, sir?"

"Just fucking do it. *Whatever's necessary.*"

"Yes Mr Culpepper," Shoe bobbed his head and retreated out of the office as quickly as his short legs would take him.

The actual trouble was one not even Shoe fully appreciated. It wasn't that £20 million was missing. Yes, that was embarrassing and yes, that may cost the Bank some customers, but the Chairman knew he could ride that difficult horse. No, it was the prospective bad debt that he'd hidden and if someone in authority started snooping around too much and that came to light then all hell was going to break loose. The mere thought gave him nightmares...

Culpepper started as someone rapped on his window. It took him a moment to focus on the policeman leaning down to stare in. He buzzed the window down.

"Are you all right sir?" the policeman asked.

Culpepper forced a smile. "I'm fine officer, thank you."

"Then perhaps you wouldn't mind moving on. You're on double yellows."

"Sorry, I only stopped for a moment."

"Well don't let me hold you up sir."

Culpepper buzzed the window shut and twisted the key in the ignition. Hiding the look of pure fury on his face he put the car into gear and drove away.

An Unexpected Reprieve

I'm sitting on a park bench, a slight breeze on my face as I watch the mundane world go by. I see fat people shoving food in their addicted mouths, sweaty joggers burning off guilty calories, animated business people talking or tapping away on their phones doing the deals of their lives, young people walking arm in arm laughing without a care in the world, shuffling old people with only arthritic dogs for company and the weight of the past on their shoulders and no future before them. I'd give my left arm to be any one of them, everyone seems to be in a more enviable position than me.

I flip open my phone, dial Claire's number and listen to the ringtone. It quickly drops into voicemail and again Claire's recorded lilt tells me to fuck off. I've tried, but failed, to get hold of her a couple of times already to see if she wants to get together tonight and give me chance to apologise for something I haven't done (again). Clearly she's not interested. Well, fuck her too.

At the time the whole Tourette's episode had felt stunningly funny, but now the urge has passed I wonder what I've done and why I've done something that is absolutely not like me. What in the hell was I thinking?

My phone rings, startling me. I check the screen but it's not Claire calling me back apologising for missing me and to profess her undying love. Instead it's Hershey. I sigh deeply, let it ring twice more until I can't avoid the inevitable any longer.

"Hi Hershey."

"Where are you?" Hershey demands. No hello, no pleasantries.

"At lunch."

"Well I suggest you get your ass back to the office immediately or you're fucking history."

The connection is unceremoniously cut.

"Shit," I say, drawing a glare from a passer-by. My talent for pissing people off is clearly at its zenith today.

Half an hour later I'm outside Hershey's office. More accurately I'm standing in the antechamber facing Hershey's hard-arse gatekeeper, Elodie. Hershey isn't keen on unapproved visitors and Elodie, a thirty-year-old buxom, bottle-blonde Parisian with flawless skin, underemphasised make-up and an arse score of 7 (despite my reservations) exercises the letter of Hershey's law to infinitesimal detail.

The rumour around the office is Elodie is incapable of counting beyond ten unless she brings her toes into play. However, as you can tell from the above description, she remains employed because of her grit and tits rather than her numeracy skills. Every male understands Hershey's reasoning, whereas not a single female employee can. Elodie is therefore universally lusted after or loathed depending upon the chromosomic and/or sexual orientation of the person staring down her fulsome top.

Except me, that is.

I don't like Elodie much, not just because she's French (which is a good enough reason) but because there's another rumour around the office, that she's fucking Hershey, and anyone prepared to get sweaty with that man isn't up to much in my opinion, huge tits or not.

"You can go straight in," says Elodie, in a tone dripping with disdain. Despite years living the right side of the Channel her accent is still heavy with garlic and snails. She grimaces a smile at me, which is not a pleasant sight I can tell you. I take great satisfaction in neglecting to point out the piece of lettuce stuck in her teeth.

"Must I?"

Elodie ignores my sarcasm and taps away at her keyboard as if I no longer exist. I wonder if Hershey really is shagging her. As I walk past Elodie mumbles something in French under her breath. It sounds a bit like she's swearing at me.

I enter Hershey's office, all dark wood and thick carpet, books (unread), glass and copious amounts of natural light, so I know he isn't a vampire. He's sitting upright, an attack dog just staring at me, unblinking, utterly unimpressed and absolutely ready to bite my head off and spit it out at the slightest provocation.

"Sit!" he barks, keeping up the dog analogy.

I sit in a hard chair facing a desk the size of Alaska, its surface unsullied by useless stuff like paperwork, only a computer screen which is blank and lifeless, as cold as a gravestone. I'm surprised nails hadn't been hammered through the seat to spike my backside in some sort of ancient religious torture. I shift my body in an attempt to look relaxed, my arms and legs open and a slight slouch to my torso, but I'm sensible enough to keep the smile off my face.

"What's this all about, Hershey?" I ask, an innocent man.

Hershey slams his palms on the desk surface and jerks to his feet, my words a rocket up his arse that cracks the wafer-thin veneer of control he had been exercising.

"As if you don't fucking know." His spittle contaminates the lovely clean desk. "I've just had the Chairman of this Bank screaming down the phone at me about your behaviour."

"Behaviour?" After years with Claire I'm well practiced at suggesting a sub zero IQ.

"Fucking Tourette's. What were you thinking?"

"Oh. That."

"Yes, that. Fuck!" says Hershey, entirely missing the irony of his own uncontrolled profanities.

He stalks over to the massive window and stares out of it, probably not seeing the magnificent view of the city. He runs his fingers through his hair as if to draw the tension out of his body, but he probably just succeeds in plastering his digits with gel.

"Well?" he demands again, looking at me via the glass.

I like to think I'm a straight-up sort of guy — what you see is what you get, so to speak — so I tend not to lie to my superiors. Even though I loathe Hershey with a passion, I still have my moral code. So I only speak to him when necessary, respond only to the questions he asks and offer no more than the absolutely needed (for this read, be economic with the truth). But as I consider his question a rare moment of candour strikes me and I decide to express my thoughts in full for once. Or perhaps it's an 'Oh fuck it' kind of day.

"I've thought about it a lot, but actually, Hershey, I really haven't a clue what came over me," I hear myself say.

Hershey's open-mouthed reflection stares at me. I can clearly see he has a gold filling. I guess that of all the answers he'd anticipated, this one would be deep down in the relegation zone of the Orkneys shuffle ball league (okay, I struggled to think of something more obscure than this, but hell, fire me). He rotates slowly to check that the manifestation and I are actually one and the same. He flops back down in his seat — lost for words for over thirty seconds, which is another first. We stare at each other, pensioners with Alzheimer's wondering what subject we're supposed to speak about next.

"Ian wanted me to fire you," he says. For Ian, read Culpepper the Bank's omnipotent, God-like Chairman, "but I argued against it. I talked Ian down to just giving you a final verbal warning. Sorry, but it was the best I could do for you. A permanent note will go on your personnel record."

I sit in stunned silence. Hershey tried to save me? It has to be a fucking lie. We're engaged in a struggle of mutual hatred. We'd crawl over the corpses of our friends and family to ensure the other was, well, a corpse. It must be someone else that doesn't want me burned at the stake, but who? I'm fucked if I know. Suddenly I'm far too tired to figure it out. If Hershey wants my thanks he can pluck them out of my ring piece.

"Okay, can I go now?" I ask.

He waves a disgusted hand at me, like a Roman Emperor fanning away a bad smell then swivels in his chair to turn his back on me. Perhaps he wants privacy whilst he learns what the colour of his abdomen fuzz is, but I don't care. I make my escape before he changes his mind and shoot past Elodie, ignoring her sneer and getting another hint of mumbled French. I gratefully step through the lift doors and let the small metal box take me down and away from Hell.

Payback

Hershey felt empty inside. Not because Josh had got away with what should have been a sackable offence. No, it was because yet again he'd received a serious bollocking from Culpepper. Hershey was furious; it wasn't his fucking fault that Josh was an idiot! Not for the first time he felt like a mongrel that had been kicked by its faithful master. Then again, fuck it. Hershey's plan was well in motion and Culpepper would bloody suffer. But he still hurt.

Then he remembered the picture in Josh's office of the ugly girl, Claire. He could make himself feel a bit better by fucking up Josh a little more. He scooped up his phone, entered e-mail and scrolled through to locate the note that he wanted. He found the number, dialled it then pressed the phone to his ear. It took only a moment for the call to be answered.

"Claire? Hi, Hershey Valentine here..."

Serena wandered the streets. Not soliciting for business, she'd never done that, never sold her body for money. But she'd been very close to doing so. To Finch. Not that she would be doing that now. Her mind and soul were in two completely different locations. A shrill voice in a tiny, previously ignored corner of her mind screamed, '*I told you so! You wouldn't listen to me. I told you so!*' Over and over and over. Serena wanted the voice to shut up but she was so disgusted with herself she let it carry on unchecked.

Her feet began to hurt; heels really weren't made for a ten-mile hike. She sat down on the nearest bench, slipped her right shoe off then massaged her foot briefly. She did the same with the other, all the time allowing herself to be scolded.

Time to go home, she thought. *I may as well beat myself up on the train as on the street.*

She checked her watch. If she hurried she could just about make it. Maybe even avoid the rain cloud that was looming.

I told you so. I told you so. I told you so...

It was starting to get a bit overcast so Jack decided it was time to leave, no point in getting wet and then a cold. A quick flick at his watch told Jack he had enough time to get to the station. Provided the bloody thing hadn't stopped working again. He lifted his watch to his ear. It was definitely ticking, which made a nice change.

Not You Again

I feel very lucky. I've taken a kicking but somehow managed to come through without any serious damage. Really my career should be on life support, with HR deciding whether to pull the plug or not. It seems like everyone is looking at me, which I know is crap, but nevertheless I have to get out of the Bank. As long as the profits flow timekeeping isn't generally questioned so nobody notices anything out of the ordinary when I bug out. It feels weird sitting on the train an hour and a half early. I undo my tie, screw it up and shove my badge of office in my briefcase. I know I'll have been successful in life when I don't have to wear a watch, a tie or socks ever again; it'll mean I won't give a shit what the time is any more, I won't have to present myself to others again and I'll be living somewhere permanently warm. But that's a dim (and highly unlikely) future.

It's stupid really because I'll have nothing to do once I get home, no one to see and nowhere to go. I've given up calling Claire. I stare absently out the window at the deserted platform, not really seeing anything. Soon it will be a seething mass of commuters but for now it's as quiet as a graveyard.

"Hey mate!" I hear someone say in a loud tone that drips familiarity.

I look up and barely suppress a groan. It's the flash-looking bloke from the trip in this morning. Just my fucking luck, what a cap to the day.

"You all right, Josh? You look terrible!" he says, looming over me.

"Oh, hi..." The synapses in my paralysed brain aren't firing and I can't dredge his name up so I guess, "...Jake."

"Jack," he corrects me with an unconcerned smile. "Mind if I...?" He waves at the empty seat opposite me, then sits down before I can respond, not looking the slightest bit upset that I got his name wrong.

"Sorry," I say, "looooong day." I can't help but feel guilty.

Jack holds up his hand and shrugs, "No biggie." The train chooses that moment to jerk into motion.

"Good or bad?" he asks.

"What?"

"Day. Good or bad?"

"The fucking worst. Right at the top of the shit list. Yours?"

"Same old, same old. Just a dull day making money, but that's import/export for you."

"Right." I nod at him as if I have an iota of interest in what he'd just said. Which I don't.

Normally I open up relatively easily to people; it's one of the aspects of my personality Claire hates. She's an introverted character who only shows herself once she's got to know and trust the other person, which can take rather an extended period.

Talking of extended periods Jack and I sit in silence for five minutes, shaking slightly from side to side with the motion of the train. He keeps smiling at me like a cheerful corpse, nodding occasionally as if responding to some unheard commentary. Right now my brain is an iceberg. My hidden depths are as cold, dark and remote as the Marianas Trench. Not a damn thing is flowing within my skull.

Jack eventually breaks the silence and says, "So what are you up to at the weekend?"

"No idea," I reply. It's Tuesday for fuck's sake, Friday night seems a mile or two away. But the reality is I'm just reluctant to say that I've probably no one to spend my leisure time with. I can tell Jack is bursting to tell me something so instead I revert to being a polite Englishman and ask, "You?"

"I'm having a load of friends over for a huge party!" he blurts out, grinning inanely.

"Sounds great," I lie.

"Oh it will be! Everyone's really cool, I've a pool, copious amounts of alcohol and there will be girls." Jack mimes each key word — glasses for cool, swimming for the pool, drinking for alcohol and curves for the girls. With a theatrical pursing of his lips he pauses as if something has occurred to him. Then he says, "If you've nothing to do why don't you come along?"

I can't think of anything worse and I hate myself as my stupid mouth says, "I may just do that." Blunt and aggressive aren't my strong suits.

"Great, I'll give you my address." And true to his word, Jack pulls out a pen (a Mont Blanc, of course), scribbles on a scrap of paper he produces from the same inside pocket and then hands it over ceremoniously. Despite myself I glance at it and cock an eyebrow. Jack's house is in the wealthiest part of town. "Arrive whatever time you want from two onwards," he says. "No earlier though. I need time to get the beers properly chilled."

"Sure," I say and slide his address into my briefcase. He nods, evidently pleased with me and pleased with himself.

Another five minutes pass in silence. Houses whizz by. When I say 'whizz' I really mean 'crawl'. Like time. *Sloooowwww.*

"What do you get up to when you're not at work?" Jack asks eventually. Perhaps he's used the intervening period to think up a couple of questions.

"Not a lot."

I'm trying to sound non-committal, but it comes out defensive. As I've already said (several times) I've no friends of my own anymore and when Claire's not around, which is often these days, not a great deal to do. Like a lot of people I tend to live a solo life reading, listening to music, surfing the web, watching television or playing games. I used to be quite a social animal but I've grudgingly noticed I spend more time on my own than ever before, hidden in my office, in splendid isolation on the train or nestled in my flat. A compartmentalised life, cushy but ultimately lonely.

"Come on, don't be so evasive," Jack cajoles me. "Tell me your passions!"

I say the first thing that pops into my head. "Cheese."

Jack is completely unfazed by my attempt at sarcasm, like being a Stilton fan is perfectly normal, and pushes me for more. "Uh-huh, aaand...?"

This time I think about it. "Beer."

"Now I can relate to that! Kronenbourg's my favourite."

I shake my head. He's a fucking halfwit. "Not lager, bitter — real ales. Lots more flavour than cold, fizzy, pissy lager."

"Really? I thought bitter was for old codgers." Jack rubs his chin, apparently thinking. "Nope, I don't think I've ever drunk any."

"There's a great pub near me, always has a new beer on. I love going there. Well...I used to anyway."

"You don't go there anymore?"

I shake my head. "My girlfriend doesn't like pubs. She prefers wine bars."

"That sounds a bit wrong to me. Does your girlfriend decide everything you do?"

"Pretty much, yes." I surprise myself when I say that and I think about it for a moment. She fucking does all right.

Jack looks incredulous. "Okay."

"Well, when I say everything, I don't really mean *everything*. I was joking." I laugh but it doesn't sound very convincing, even to me.

"Where's your girlfriend?"

"At work."

"So, come out for a beer then. Tonight."

"I can't," I say desperately. This is getting worse, first a party and now a drink. "We're doing something."

"What?"

"I don't know yet."

"Because she hasn't told you?"

I shrug, trying to regain some balance, tipping a bit with the weight of Jack's words and my own thoughts.

"You know," Jack says, all philosophical like, "it's always best to ask for forgiveness, rather than permission. No one ever got a bollocking for doing the right thing."

"What book did you get that one from?"

"The book of life." Honest to God, I kid you not, that's what the twat said. He goes on before I can comment, "What's the pub called?"

"What?"

"The pub. The one you like going to?"

I tell him, my mind on the aspects of my relationship that Jack has been poking his grubby fingers into.

"Maybe I'll go there sometime and try a beer."

"Good idea. You do that."

I turn away to look out the window and watch the last of the grimy terraced houses slide by. They look like they haven't been cleaned since the days of steam. I see clothes fluttering on washing lines, children bouncing on trampolines, an old man leaning over a fence smoking.

Normal. Dull. Like me.

I hope my rudeness has dead-ended the conversation because I just want to be by myself, to wallow in my own shit called Claire. I don't need a chirpy moron yacking in my ear and adding to the clutter in the particular pit I'm residing in. But it's not to be, as Jack again proves to be a relentless machine spewing out inane chatter from a mouth that never seems to close. I won't bore you with the crap he spouts as it would fill a hundred pages and this book would rightly end up in the bin or deleted but, bizarrely, as the train pushes into Kent I begin to warm to him and I start to respond. Nothing either of us says is particularly profound, but there's no challenge in him, no competitive banking bullshit, no politics, no one-upmanship, just talk for the sake of it which seems to be enough for both of us. Eighty-five minutes later the train pulls into Ramsgate and Jack gets off. He waves cheerfully at me through the window. I nod back, thinking it's been a long time since I've just *chatted* to someone.

"Broadstairs. The next stop is Broadstairs," the pre-recorded voice announces over the tannoy.

I plug my iPod into my ears. My aching brain needs to switch off and a blast of heavy, thudding music at an extreme volume will probably help. Two minutes of crawling at wheelchair pace and the train draws up, only one more stop to go before I too can step off and retreat into my flat. I've seen the dinky little platform hundreds, maybe thousands of times so I barely glance out of the window. The scarcely known band Cage the Elephant wail in my ears about stuff 'going in one ear and out of the other', which is fucking apt really.

Then, out of the corner of my eye I see a flash of platinum blonde. I whip my head around and yes, it's the girl from this morning walking past my window. She looks rather pale and deep in thought, but nevertheless still pretty stunning. Without thinking about it I rap on the window to get her attention. She looks at me blankly, no recognition there, nothing at all in her blue eyes, then she gazes down at her shoes, not breaking her stride in the slightest. The train jerks into motion, gathers a tiny bit of speed and she's gone. I crane my neck to keep sight of her, but the platform is empty, like she never existed.

I feel momentarily embarrassed. What was I thinking trying to get the attention of such a stunner? And me in a deep and meaningful relationship. Every now and again this happens to me. Let's call it a 'condition'. I see a girl and I'm instantly attracted to her. But I never do anything about it. Give up eight years for a quick shag? I can't do it, because I'm too loyal to Claire. I know how I'd feel if positions were reversed and I found out my partner had been screwing around. It'd fucking kill me. However, another part of my mind tells me in a quiet voice that perhaps I could be in a better relationship.

"Shut the fuck up."

I realise a tad late that I've spoken out loud. Not a moment too soon and I'm off the train as well, glad to remove myself from where I've managed to humiliate myself. Again.

As I'm exiting the station the train vibrates past me and drifts along the track in a fug of ionised air. The weather is still good, quite balmy really. The Isle of Thanet is surrounded by the sea on three sides so it has its own little microclimate ('micro' means little I guess). Legend has it (don't ask me how I know this shit) that 2,000 years ago Thanet was known as the Isle of the Dead. The French (Gauls to be accurate) believed the spirits of the dead were rowed here and ceremoniously deposited by Le Grim Reaper (who probably wore a stripy top, had strings of onions wrapped around his neck and regularly went on strike). So even then we had bloody immigrants flooding the place. Some things never change, even over millennia.

I peel my jacket off and throw it over my shoulder, in an attempt at a 'devil can fuck off' look as I exit the train station. Straight in front of me is Buenos Aires. The mad Russian is nowhere in sight. Maybe he's earned enough cash from robbing passers-by to consider going home for lobster and foie gras with a glass of Cristal. I severely doubt he's been nicked or even moved on by the local rozzers. Thanet is the equivalent of an elephant boneyard for the boys in blue — this is where you're sent to die after a particularly big fuck-up, or if you're just plain shite at your job. Arresting miscreants isn't the issue, doing the paperwork is.

Just then my mobile rings. I look at the screen, sigh heavily and briefly consider ignoring it, but I can't. "Hi Claire."

"I won't be home tonight," she says. No pleasantries then.

"Why?" I ask bluntly. Two can play this childish little game.

"I'm having dinner with a prospect I've been after for ages. It'll be a late one so I'll stay up town."

"Bit late notice isn't it?" I'm not happy and a pissy tone creeps into my voice. I know it'll annoy her and create more tension between us, but I just can't help myself.

"There's not much I can do about that," she replies with an audible shrug. She may as well have said, *Fuck you.* "It was all last minute and it's too big an opportunity to miss. It'll be really good for my career if I bring it in."

Ah, the career, the ace card. I play relationship, she raises and sees me with vocation. If we get through this then I expect one day others such as 'marriage', 'body clock' and maybe 'divorce' will be pressed into service. The idea of a series of life-events with Claire creates a surprising shiver of fear inside me.

"What am I going to do with myself then?" I cringe inside as soon as I blurt it out because I'm doing exactly what Jack predicted, asking for permission.

"For fuck's sake Josh. It's always the same with you. Do I have to make *every* decision for you?"

"No," I say weakly.

But Claire doesn't hear me as she carries on full steam with the rant. "How about play with yourself? Get pissed? What do I care? You're a grown-up, work it out for yourself."

"Maybe I'll do both." I say with a further bout of childish petulance.

I hear an exasperated sigh at the other end of the phone. It's been a very long day and I simply don't want to mire myself any more in it, so I roll over and play dead. "Whatever Claire. Enjoy yourself."

"It's just business so I can assure you there will be no enjoyment involved," she chides me. "See you some time." She disconnects the call before I have the chance to retort.

Shedding Skin

Jack leant against his door, forcing the Yale lock to snap into place with a loud click. It was a habit. Every time he heard the sound he knew he was home, that he could drop the charade and go back to being himself. It was hard work, pretending, having to be something he wasn't. But then he figured that millions of people did the same thing as him every day. They pretended to colleagues at work, pretended to wives, girlfriends, boyfriends, husbands, parents at home. Pretended to mates in the pub, strangers on the street, associates on the train.

Today he'd made an acquaintance. Or had the guy he'd met on the train been lying too? His gut told him he hadn't been. Could they become friends? Jack hoped so, because if it were true Jack knew he would do anything — *anything* — to ensure they grew to become friends and stayed that way.

Pushing himself off the door he walked down the corridor, dropping his briefcase, then his jacket on the floor. As he went the tie and shirt followed. He had to hop on one leg and then the next as the trousers came off.

"We're all fucking liars," Jack said to himself as he switched the kettle on clad only in socks and Y-fronts.

Taking his suit off was like peeling away a second skin, becoming himself again.

And he hated who he was.

Приветствия!

A short ten minute stroll along the seafront and I'm home, in my flat in the old town. The original part of Margate is supposed, one day, to be seeing a renaissance whenever they start to build the proposed art gallery literally across the road from me. The old town is a reasonably pleasant area with a record shop and a handful of pubs (one a shithole) in the space of a few hundred yards. There's even a comic shop for the geeks out there. But outside this green zone you're back on the frontline of the chav.

The flat itself is reasonably pleasant, with high ceilings and the feeling of plenty of space. We've two bedrooms (useful for guests crashing out pissed or, more likely these days, to retreat into after an argument), a kitchen diner, living room and a decent-sized bathroom. For Margate the rent is high, for the south east of England it's a steal. It's where I live and sometimes where Claire stays with me. The flat is full of her stuff but she's never officially been willing to move in, keeping her own place in London and staying either with me or her parents when hanging locally. I'm more of a weekend haunt for Claire these days.

I slam the front door to piss off the neighbours (who've four bastard kids that are so loud my ceiling seems to be made of rice paper) but mainly in an effort to make myself feel better after the call with Claire. The noise reverberates along the corridor, which all the rooms lead off, before dying as fast as it was born, like my brief and sadistic enjoyment.

I toss my bag and jacket onto the bed as I pass by. They bounce off the mattress and onto the floor. I stop in my tracks mid-thud. All the doors along the corridor are open which isn't right because I'd closed them myself this morning before I left. Either Claire is playing a joke and is in the flat or, more likely, I've been robbed. I march the length of the corridor and glance briefly into each room — the other bedroom, bathroom, cupboard, living room. Everything looks present and in its place. Then I'm in the kitchen and walking straight into Konstantin, about as complete a surprise as I can imagine.

The tramp flashes me a toothless grin. In one hand he holds a half-drunk bottle from my Gadd's stash and in the other the wallet (empty I expect) that he stole from me half a day ago. He raises the beer bottle in a salute.

"Nasdrovia." he says and downs the rest of the contents.

Just when I think the day can't get any weirder.

Starters

Claire felt uncomfortable to say the least. Her prospective client was already late and she was struggling to hold the table in the popular restaurant owned by a celebrity chef. Two glasses of wine to steady her nerves had already been ordered and consumed and she was feeling distinctly light-headed. She had deliberately picked the place because, in her view, it was a classy joint and Josh would never dream of bringing her here, so she pulled a double whammy — a decent (free) night out and a big contract that would win her plaudits. Claire was sure Patricia would even forego the bollocking for overstepping her expenses budget in what would be a colossal style.

She checked her make-up in a small hand mirror for at least the fifth time. Normally she didn't wear any, but she wanted to make an effort so she'd layered on foundation, eyeliner and lipstick. She'd also borrowed a designer dress from a friend. It was low-cut but she had, like many of the London-based financial institutions, limited assets to display. A few bunches of toilet paper had helped boost her chest but she was paranoid that the white tissue would rise up and stand out in sharp contrast to the black fabric.

The waiter was walking over to her again. *Oh fuck,* she thought. She'd asked him for five more minutes ten minutes ago.

"Madam," the waiter said smoothly, "your guest has arrived."

Claire sighed with relief as the waiter moved to one side, pulled out a chair and allowed the tall man following him to sit down. Hershey Valentine reached across to shake her hand. His grip was surprisingly strong. Interesting. In her experience men were usually afraid to apply any pressure when greeting a woman.

"It's a pleasure to meet you at last, Claire," he drawled in a voice louder than it needed to be. "Sorry I'm late." He grinned disarmingly.

A good-looking bastard and knows it, Claire thought immediately.

"No problem at all, Mr Valentine," she smiled, "I've only just arrived myself."

She was relieved that the waiter had the good grace to just about keep a straight face through the lie.

"Please, call me Hershey," he said.

"Sir, madam, welcome to Chez Chez. What would you like to drink?" the waiter interrupted.

"A Chardonnay, Californian, lightly-oaked," Hershey replied.

"An *excellent* choice, and for you madam, the rosé again?"

Claire blushed as Hershey eyed the empty wine glass in front of her. She was either busted as a liar or he considered her a lush.

"Just a mineral water please," Claire said.

"No way," Hershey said. "She'll have the same as me."

The waiter looked at Claire. *Fuck it, why not?* she thought and nodded in agreement.

The waiter whisked away her soiled glass then disappeared. Hershey turned his full, radiant attention on her.

"Well, it's a pleasure to be meeting at last," he boomed.

"I thought you were avoiding me," Claire replied, sounding more churlish than she'd wanted to. A gentle-humoured reproach was all she'd been aiming for.

Hershey looked pissed off. *Shit, shit!* Claire screamed in her mind. She wished she'd taken that mineral water now.

"Not at all!" he grinned, the grimace gone as quickly as it had appeared. "I've just been real busy, that's all. You know how it is."

"But you're free now, which is great!"

The waiter returned with two unsullied wine glasses which he placed reverentially in front of them whilst another waiter, who seemed to be cloned from the first, placed a bucket next to the table, the ice clinking in a hollow rattle. One clone retreated whilst the other tugged the bottle out of the bucket, drops of water tumbling off it.

"Would madam care to try first?" he asked.

Normally Claire couldn't give a shit about the taste of a wine and was untutored in grape, terroir and structure alike, but she rightly suspected just diving in would look rude and uncouth in front of such an obviously cultured man who had, after all, been born on another continent and reached a lofty position in a prominent institution. So she said, "Yes, please."

The waiter dribbled a small quantity of piss-coloured liquid into Claire's glass, then stepped back and nonchalantly glanced around the room as if he was politely ignoring Claire.

She took a small sip and nodded. "Very nice," she said, surprised that she'd spoken the truth.

Claire's metaphorical invisibility over and done with, the waiter returned his gaze to her and nodded with abject delight. He topped up her glass then poured a decent quantity into Hershey's globe before slipping away to blend in with the wallpaper.

Claire wasn't sure how to start the conversation and Hershey, who was more intent on casting an appraising eye over his fellow diners, clearly didn't want to initiate anything. Her difficulty was momentarily deferred by the ceremonial delivery of the menu, which looked as if it had been handwritten by the chef on expensive, thick vellum. It even had gold braid attached, for fuck's sake. Claire and Hershey silently scanned the selections.

"Are you a starter or a dessert person?" she asked with just her eyes peeking over the top of the menu.

"Huh?" Hershey said, by the look on his face clearly puzzled by the question.

"You know, do you prefer to have either a starter or a dessert as well as your main course?"

"You mean I have to *choose*?"

"No," Claire laughed, "it's just I normally have a dessert, chocolate preferably, and I need to leave room for it so I skip the starter."

Hershey looked somewhat stunned. "In America we eat all three courses with maybe another one thrown in."

"Oh. I guess that explains why you're all so obese!"

Hershey glared at her and she cursed herself for putting a foot wrong yet again so early in the process of wooing a new account.

"Not everyone in America is overweight you know," he admonished.

"Well I can tell you're not!" she laughed lightly.

Hershey grimaced a smile in return. He'd had to remind himself several times already why he was here and why he needed to stick it out with this clearly loathsome woman, regardless of what she said or did. He scanned the menu again, using the moment to quash his irritation. A minute later the waiter reappeared to take their order. Hershey looked at Claire with a little surprise when she ordered a starter and main course.

"Not saving yourself for dessert?" he asked with the merest niggle of sarcasm.

She shook her head. "I decided to follow your advice. I figured, what the hell."

Hershey nodded in apparent appreciation and then ordered himself. The waiter bobbed his head to show he'd understood, retreated and silence descended again. As Hershey gazed around the room Claire took the opportunity to look him over. She had to admit he was relatively good-looking, not really her type, but nevertheless there were some attributes (like a lean body and a global view) that she could appreciate.

So very different to Josh...

"Do you mind me asking why you suddenly decided to get in touch?" she asked, fed up with the silence. She chose not to mention the swear-word-laden e-mail she'd received from Hershey earlier in the day.

Hershey leisurely returned his attention to her. "My secretary screwed up," he lied. "I told her to get in touch with you. When I realised she'd failed to do so I did it myself."

"I hope you fired her!" Claire joked.

"I did," Hershey said with a completely straight face.

"Oh!"

She wasn't sure whether to believe the loud American or not and Hershey clearly wasn't going to tell her. Fortunately the waiter appeared with a small sorbet as a precursor to the starter ("To cleanse the palette."). She dipped the tiny spoon provided into the icy bulge and savoured the flavour (water melon) that liquefied on her tongue, instantly losing any consideration of the unfortunate secretary who'd been sacrificed for her career. *Ah well, fuck her*, she thought.

"Rather...delicate," Hershey said.

He speaks with a very strident voice, Claire thought for a second time.

"Yes, I do," replied Hershey.

"That was out loud wasn't it?" Claire asked.

Hershey nodded.

"Shit!"

"Don't sweat it," Hershey shrugged, a smile on his face. "It's a national trait of ours."

"Is it?" she smiled back. She felt as if the ice had at least cracked.

"Sure! Listen," Hershey said, leaning over. Claire followed suit. "We citizens of the US of A have eleven times more space than you English guys so we have to raise our voices a little to make ourselves heard."

Claire laughed. This time Hershey smiled with her. "Actually," he continued, "if truth be told my father was an army colonel. He always shouted and we kids learned to do the same."

The waiter stretched an arm into their huddle to whisk away the sorbet dishes and replace them with their starters. Claire tucked in. She was beginning to feel much more comfortable in the brash American's company. He was proving very different to all the rumours.

Take My Number

"What the fuck are you doing in my flat?" I demand.

The Russian grins. An explosive belch ejects a spicy cloud in my direction. Konstantin, unperturbed, yanks open my fridge and pulls out another beer.

"You want?" he says in heavily-accented English and offers me the bottle.

Fuck it, why not drink one of my own beers? I think.

I stick out a hand but first he levers off the cap using his teeth. He presses the chilled bottle into my palm. It's damp to the touch. I wipe the neck with my sleeve. He digs into the fridge again and reappears with one for himself and repeats his party trick.

"I Konstantin Boryakov," he says. My new best friend clinks his bottle on mine, raises it in a salute and there's a moment's pause as we both take a deep draught. The cold beer hits the back of my throat, then my stomach. A belch of my own clambers up from the depths. For a moment I pause, expecting Claire to complain as she always does when any gas escapes one of my orifices. But of course she isn't in the flat, there's just a Russian tramp grinning like a maniac.

"How did you get in?" I ask.

Konstantin holds up a couple of pieces of short metal, bent at the end. "I pick lock," he admits.

"Oh."

"I here return wallet," he says and holds out the cheap canvas case I'd handed over this morning. I put it down on the small dining table in the corner. It feels thin (i.e. empty). I don't bother to look inside.

"Trying to save me money?"

The Russian looks puzzled. "Why I care?" he shrugs. "I know you wealthy boy."

"Good point."

Konstantin gives me an 'I told you so' nod then pushes off the work surface he's leaning on and limps past me. I follow, a compliant sheep. The tramp walks the few feet along the corridor to my living room.

"You know your way around then," I say.

It's intended as sarcasm, but he seems to take my comment gravely. He shrugs again then flops down on my pristine white sofa. I cringe inside at the state the cushions will be in when he lifts his dirty arse off them.

"Is important know your territory," he says heavily.

"What are you, a spy?" I laugh.

"Da," Konstantin replies with another shrug, "but I no kill people for Mother Russia no more."

I choke off my laugh and drop down into the armchair facing my grubby could-be assassin.

"Are you going to kill me?" I ask with an audible gulp.

Konstantin laughs so hard he must surely bust a rib. He slaps a grimy hand on his thigh as loudly as a snapping neck and spills some beer on the sofa in the process. Claire is going to kill me if Konstantin doesn't. After a minute of gut-wrenching mirth the Russian finally draws breath and wipes tears from his eyes.

"Kill you? You funny man! No, you be dead already if I want." He starts laughing again but I can't bring myself to join in.

"Fucking hell, is that supposed to make me feel better?"

"Aaah, no," the tramp shakes his head. "Is fact."

I drink some more beer whilst I furiously think. It's at times like these in films and thrillers where the hero (presumably, in this case, me) thinks of a brilliant plan or starts a fight with a newspaper, but Tom Cruise and Matt Damon I am not. Besides, I haven't read the latest FHM yet. I don't want to get it covered in blood. Not for the first time that day my mind is an utter blank. Then a flash of inspiration hits me (better that than Konstantin's fist).

"So why aren't you a spy anymore?" I ask. Do you see my tactic? Build a rapport with your enemy, humanise yourself in their eyes. I read it in a thriller once.

"No your business," he says whilst a granite expression settles swiftly on his face.

"Oh." My tactic dies a death there and then. I just hope I'm not going to as well.

He roars with laughter and slaps his thigh again. "You funny guy."

I don't have a fucking clue why he thinks I'm so hilarious and frankly, prospective death threat or no, I'm getting pretty fed up of being laughed at by a crusty old tramp. I take a huge gulp of beer to steel myself.

"So what do you want?" I ask, my tone more blancmange than steel.

"Me? I want help."

Which is the last thing I expect to hear.

"What do you expect me to do for you?" I ask in an incredulous voice. "You already help yourself to my cash regularly."

Konstantin shakes his head. "No, you mistaken," he says. "*Me* help *you,* funny man. Repaying debt important in my country. Is matter of *honour.*"

Which puzzles me as the Russian obviously doesn't have two pennies to rub together and I've given him a *lot* of cash. Clearly my lack of understanding is plastered all over my face because Konstantin says, "You in trouble, da." A statement, not a question.

I shake my head, "No, not at all."

"Da. You in *biiig* trouble."

"Look, I'd know if I was in fucking trouble and I'm fucking not, all right?" I'm starting to get mightily pissed off with everyone apparently knowing me better than I do.

"So you know you followed?"

"Huh? I don't know have a clue what you're talking about."

"This morning, man in taxi. He watch you. I watch him."

"Nope, still don't have a clue what the fuck you're saying."

Konstantin ignores my petulance. "Which is why I here. Man follow this morning, he follow all week."

"Man?"

"Da, man! Wear suit, grey hair, blank look. Spy, like me. But not as good." He laughs again. "This I know. Fact."

"Sorry, still no idea what you're talking about."

"Then you need find out what he about," Konstantin advises in a hard voice. He stands, drains his beer and gives me the empty bottle as he passes. "See you round," he says and pats me on the cheek. "If you not dead first."

A moment later the front door bangs shut and Konstantin is gone, but he's left his mark, literally, behind him. I sit for a long moment nursing my Gadd's and wondering what the hell has just happened. The room feels larger without Konstantin, like he's taken up three times more space than the size of his body. Or maybe it was just his smell that had. I get up and open a window. Immediately salty sea air whistles in, bringing with it the sounds of light traffic and heavy seagulls (bastards, I hate them nearly as much as I hate the French). I carry the empty bottles into the kitchen, then throw the cushion covers (which stink, by the way) into the washing machine and turn it on. It's a half-hearted attempt to tidy up for Claire. She might not live here but life is too short for yet another bust-up in my life.

I see the empty wallet on the table out of the corner of my eye. I pick it up and glance inside. It isn't quite empty, in fact. In the section intended to hold banknotes is a piece of white paper. I tug it out and unfold it. It isn't a cheque for untold thousands of pounds but a note. In a neat script is an eleven-digit number and the letter K. Ah, the modern age when even penniless tramps living on the street can own mobile phones.

"What the *fuck* is going on?" I ask.

He's Just Dull

"Do you have a sweetheart?" Hershey asked through a mouthful of food. 'Sweetheart' wasn't a word he usually used (he'd struggled to think of a suitable phrase) and it made an unusual shape in his mouth. He was more accustomed to others like 'loose' and 'easy' but he particularly liked the English word 'slapper'. So lyrical.

Claire was taken completely off guard. "No. Yes. Well, maybe," she said, flustered, her mind racing.

Hershey laughed. It sounded like grated cheese, soft and pointless. "Which is it? Yes, no or maybe?"

Claire put her spoon down with a sigh that came from the depths of her soul. "Honestly Hershey? I don't know. We've been together a long time and probably that's the only reason we still are."

"It's easy?" asked Hershey.

She nodded, wondering why she was being so open with someone she barely knew and had only just met. But a dam had burst in her mind and all these words came tumbling out in a torrent of emotion.

"Well it was, but it's just fucking *dull* now. We don't do anything exciting, don't go anywhere. Anyone vaguely interesting has moved to London but Josh insists on staying in bloody Margate! Who *chooses* to live in Margate?"

"Margate? Where's that?"

"Just some seaside shithole in Kent," she replied, but she could see by Hershey's shrug he didn't even know what or where Kent was. "We don't have fun anymore. Our sex life is non-existent, we haven't fucked for months. When we did used to do it the sex was always over before you knew it. Sixty seconds from cuddle to puddle."

"Is that all?" Hershey asked lightly.

The sarcasm passed Claire by, an unseen pedestrian in a pea-souper. "And he wants *children*." She shuddered visibly. "Who in their right mind wants to shove an eight-pound lump of flesh *out* of their vagina for fuck's sake? It's unnatural."

She sat back in her chair, out of breath. Hershey let her calm down for a few moments, pleased at the rapid turn of events and surprised he'd had to do so little to engineer them.

"Do you think he's having an affair?"

She shook her head. "No, he's too unimaginative for that. He's like a dog sitting faithfully at my heel. When I say 'roll over' he does."

"What's wrong with that?" Hershey asked, genuinely puzzled. "Sounds like an ideal relationship to me."

Claire wasn't listening. "I just want him to...react, I guess. To do something unexpected."

"Uh-huh. And what do you plan to do about it?"

She looked up at Hershey, as if seeing him for the first time, as if realising she had been speaking out loud for the first time.

"Excuse me?" she said.

"In my world if there's a problem or an opportunity, you deal with it or act on it," he said.

Claire took a large swig of wine, emptying the glass. She topped it up again and had another swallow before banging it back down with a huge sigh.

"Christ, I don't know. I really don't know."

Hershey leant over the table and took her hand. "Yes you do."

She drank some more wine, staring into the middle distance. Hershey waved at a clone waiter, pointing to the empty bottle.

"It was the same for me one time," Hershey said in a soft voice, squeezing her hand.

"What was?"

For fuck's sake, you thick bitch, Hershey thought, but said instead, "My relationship, so I know exactly what you mean. We were dead on the inside, but on the outside no one knew what state we were really in. We just kept on going for the sake of it, because everyone expected it of us. We were the ideal couple who had it all."

"What happened in the end?"

Hershey paused for a moment, a pained expression flashing across his face.

"She dumped me for someone else."

"What a fucking *bitch*!" she said, loud enough for one or two heads to turn and frown at her.

"I thought so at the time, but looking back I'd agree with her now."

"Really?"

"Yeah, frankly I was a boring bastard, I'd got stuck in a rut. That way of life shouldn't be for anyone. Total waste of time, both of us blew two years on something that was never going to bear fruit."

Claire nodded slowly, thinking.

"How's the salad?" Hershey asked.

"Hmm?"

He pointed his fork at her starter.

"I've no idea," she said. "I hadn't even realised I was eating."

Hershey looked at her largely empty plate with surprise.

"How's yours?" she asked.

"Crap, of course. All English food is crap, like your weather."

"What is it with you Americans?" Claire was pissed off and in the mood for a fight.

"Huh, whaddaya mean?" Hershey bristled, not used to being challenged and not appreciating it either.

"Every American I've ever met complains about being in England, so why live here? The Scots are the same. Moan, moan, fucking moan, but everywhere you turn, there's another one, and another. What I don't understand is, if home's so great is why not fuck off back there?"

Hershey forced a laugh. "God, how I *love* your English humour! Babe, I'd love to 'fuck off home' as you say, but it's my job. I just have to grin and bear your shitty little country."

Claire laughed loudly. 'Babe'. She felt a little thrill at the word. "I was only joking, Hershey, no insult intended."

"No insult taken," Hershey lied. "Here, have some more wine."

Melancholy Baby

The hour isn't late but the room is asphalt black. Konstantin's odour has finally dragged itself out of the window so the lights are off and the curtains as tightly closed as Claire's legs. I reach down and feel around for beer. On the fourth fumble I find a bottle that actually has some alcohol in it, but not for long. I lift it to my lips and drain it dry, sucking out the last drops. After Konstantin's departure I needed a drink and in large quantities. All because there's a heavy weight on my mind. A quick trip out to the off-licence had generated a threefold increase in the volume of Gadd's chilling in my fridge.

Konstantin is obviously talking utter bollocks. I simply cannot believe someone has any reason whatsoever to follow me. I'm a boring bastard with an average job. No one would want my life, therefore I can only conclude Konstantin was completely off his tits on some Class A shit. I try to shelve his comments in a dark place in my mind with all the other useless crap. But it's futile; the thoughts keep knocking at the door, wanting to be heard.

However, what's really bothering me is Claire. She's been an utter cow recently, treating me like a dog even though I can't think of anything I've done wrong. One minute our relationship is running on at a steady pace then, out of nowhere, we've skidded, gone up a bank and hit a wall. It's certainly not the first time. How many people do you know that manage to go more than a few months without a dust-up, never mind eight years? But this one is subtly different — I largely don't care how she feels.

It's said that everyone's good at something, which implies that we're terrible at lots of things. In my case clearly my downside is holding relationships together. Mentally I run back through my (relatively short) list of ex's. I thought each was a satisfactory progression along the road we all seem doomed to take — marriage, kids, old age and death, with working all the hours in between to pay for it all. Although each stage should be forwards, I've long suspected (but never admitted) that meeting Claire was a reversal. As happens periodically, my memory takes me back in time to the first two years of my degree when I was madly in love with Claire's precursor, Alison.

Alison. Wow, what a *stunner* (arse score 11). Everything about her made my heart sing and — even better — my head accompanied my beating organ in perfect harmony — that's when you know you've got it right. We'd been on the same course (economics with management studies, yawn) and I'd been smacked between the eyes the first time I saw her, on day one of university. She immediately became my morning shower wank fantasy (day two). But never did I think my solo desires would become reality, and when, amazingly, we did get together I thought we'd never split up.

Sadly I was wrong.

One-and-a-half years of pleasure and fun and then the inexplicable snapping of the relationship just before the summer holidays. I still can't remember why it happened and who broke up with whom. The final year had been tense. We had the same friends, most of who were couples now, and went to the same places, which made life difficult to say the least. In an effort to break out I'd gone to a new club in the initial couple of weeks back at university and met Claire. So to take my mind off Alison, I jumped into bed with her. I was soon immersed in Claire's life and circle of friends. Alison, to my knowledge, stayed single. We graduated, congratulated each other, then went our separate ways. I've never heard from her since, although I think of her often.

I'm rudely jerked out of my melancholia by the chime of my mobile. No flash ringtone for me, just a double beep that indicates someone has sent me a text. I pick up my phone, which is easy to find because the screen is the only bright spot in the coffin lit room. It hurts my eyes looking at it. I tap a button to open the message.

It reads, "Fancy a beer? Jack."

Ah.

Dressing Up To Go Down

Serena sat on the edge of her expansive and expensive bed, looking at herself in the floor-to-ceiling mirror. From the outside she looked fine, her uniform neat, her hair tidy. For now at least. Later it was highly likely she'd get into trouble and be mauled by some grubby guy. It happened on most shifts and she couldn't see why today would be any different after the shit she'd already taken.

She sighed heavily. It wasn't the external appearance that bothered her, it was the inside that did, the stuff she couldn't see, her husband James couldn't see, that no one could see. Except Finch. He'd looked straight into her and spotted *exactly* who she was.

The thought of Finch made her shake her head. How close she'd come to being in one of his films. Thanks to the Internet she was certain that eventually someone she'd known would have seen it and then everything she had around her would have been gone — house, car, husband, friends, life. *Everything.* Well, not quite everything. The job didn't really matter and her self-respect had evaporated *long* ago. The money was an irrelevance too. She couldn't spend everything James earned. To be accurate, James didn't *earn* his wages, no one that got paid well over seven figures a year could possibly *deserve* that amount of cash.

She decided she'd call Finch tomorrow and refuse to work for him. It's not like they had a contract or anything; Finch was just going to pay a fee every time she got on her knees. The rates would vary, of course, depending upon what she was supposed to do with her body (or more accurately certain parts of it) and with whom.

Enough, she thought. That can wait for tomorrow. Tonight she had to go to work.

Oh, If I Have To

Fucking hell, Jack again.

OK, on the way home I'd come to the conclusion that he's not such a bad guy, but that doesn't automatically make him my first choice to have a beer with. I have a digit poised in the air above my phone ready to stab at N (the second letter being O), but then I look around the room and at myself. Here I am, all on my own, drinking. I need the anaesthesia alcohol delivers to numb the extraction of two emotions — embarrassment (at my behaviour today) and fear (at the state of my relationship). But I can't stand the brooding silence and the anxiety of my own company, so I relent and type, "Where are you?"

Within a millisecond my phone pings again, like Jack had the message typed out already and was just waiting to hit the send key. I open the message. It reads, "Your favourite watering hole." There's even a little smiley icon for fuck's sake.

But it's my great little pub around the corner and I need a friendly face — even if it's a stupid one you'd just as soon punch as look at. I jump up, grab my wallet and run out of the flat. I think I hear the door shut behind me, but I'm not sure and I don't care. It's a minute's walk or a 45-second trot (okay, I'm not the fittest man in the world) from my flat. Less than 30 seconds away from my front door is another boozer, but I'd rather be infected with the Ebola virus than go inside. It's the perfect advert *against* extended opening hours. In fact, I struggle to remember a time when it's actually *been* shut. There's always at least one old soak standing outside filling his nicotine-enhanced lungs with cancerous smoke, pint glass in hand.

I push open the pub door, which jams slightly as it's literally a spit-and-sawdust place (okay, no spit but there *is* sawdust). The interior is separated into a couple of drinking areas. I prefer the front space where there are old, huge tables to place your pint, big enough to lean on without fear of pushing them over. There's always a good range of beer on tap and it changes regularly. Mind you, I struggle to remember the last time I'd been in here; Claire prefers a nearby wine bar. I've always felt far more comfortable in a place that sells alcohol in proper measures.

I look for a flash suit (none) but I can't see Jack so I head up to the bar, choose the strongest beer on the list that I haven't had before, pay for it and take a long draught. I feel a tap on my shoulder, which makes me jump an inch off the floor. Fortunately I manage to keep all the liquid contained; proudly, not a drop is spilled or sprayed.

"Hi Josh," says Jack, in casual clothes, but still well dressed.

I swallow, then cough. "For fuck's sake you scared the shite out of me!"

"Sorry," he says. "Want another one?"

"Erm, no, only just started this one thanks." I take another pull on the strong, warm brown beer to steady my nerves.

"Are you sure? It's half-gone already."

I'm about to argue then I see that he's right. "Fuck it, why not?"

He grins and stands waiting at the bar to get served whilst I grab a table. A minute later and he joins me, a beer in each hand. He raises it in the air and stares dubiously into its murky depths like one of Macbeth's witches looking for inspiration.

"Does it taste better than it looks?" he asks, some reservation in his voice.

"Only one way to find out," I reply and start on my second pint.

He hesitatingly raises the glass to his lips and takes the smallest of sips. He pulls a face like an eleven-year-old boy drinking alcohol for the first time. Kids never seem to get over this displeasure until at least, oh, thirteen or so. Then it's alcopops and cider for the next three years until lager GCSEs, snakebite A-levels, then graduating to vodka Red Bull and so on.

Neither of us speaks for at least five minutes. Jack looks around the pub, beaming at everyone and everything, periodically sipping his bitter then periodically grimacing. All I can do is stare at the surface of my diminishing pint. Finally his evident dislike for the beer gets to me.

"Look, if it's not to your taste I can get you something else," I say.

"No I'm fine, honestly," he assures me, then does the sip/grimace routine again.

Without arguing I push off the barrel I'm sitting on and go to the bar and get him a pint of scrumpy. "Try that."

"No, I'm alright."

"Jack, just take the fucking cider will you?"

He looks crestfallen, extends an arm and accepts the proffered glass, takes a mouthful, then places it next to the bitter.

"I would have been fine with the beer."

"I'm sorry," I say. "It's been a really shitty day."

"Yes, you said so on the train."

We fall silent again. I'm on the verge of leaving. What the fuck was I thinking coming here with someone I barely know and have less in common with?

"I have a confession to make," Jack admits. I look at him, eyebrows raised. "The beer does taste like shit."

For the first time that day, probably for the first time in weeks, I laugh. And laugh. And laugh. It takes me a good few minutes to calm down, as if my mind and body need a complete release.

"Thanks for that Jack," I say. He smiles in response and I can see he's clueless as to what he's done to deserve my gratitude.

"Is it girlfriend trouble?" he asks in what I suspect is a wild stab in the dark.

"It's everything trouble, mate," I say. He grins again; maybe nobody has called him 'mate' before. "But she is a big part of it, yes."

"Want to talk about it?"

"Not particularly, no."

"Good, 'cos I'm crap at all that touchy-feely stuff. I'm a treat 'em mean, keep 'em keen kinda guy."

Christ, he even uses his fingers, mimicking speech quotes, to emphasise the point in fashion that went out of date 30 years ago.

"You know you're a bit of a twat when you talk like that, Jack."

Another emotion skitters across his face. Surprise. "Oh. Really?"

"Uh-huh."

"Sorry. It's just the company I keep during the day. They're well...twats, I suppose."

I feel bad again. Jack seems like a decent guy but it's a bit difficult to tell with the thick veneer of bravado and bullshit. Time to change the subject.

"That blonde girl on the train this morning," I say.

"Yeah, what about her?"

"You seemed to know her."

"A bit, I've seen her around."

"Who is she?"

He shrugs. "No one important."

He might think nothing of the blonde but for some reason I can't get her out of my head. Jack seems to have got the taste for drink now as he pours the remains of the pint down his throat and asks, "Want another?" Without waiting for an answer he goes to the bar and waves at the landlord to get his attention.

A movement at the window catches my eye. Konstantin grins at me, points two fingers first at his eyes, then at me in an 'I'm watching you' gesture. It's then that Jack returns with two more pints and sets them down none too gently, spilling some of the precious liquid. When I look back to the window the mad Russian is gone.

"What is it with you?" he demands harshly.

"Sorry?" The character shift has caught me by surprise.

"You and women, what is it with you? One minute you're whining about your girlfriend, the next you're mooning over this blonde bint."

"I'm hardly mooning, Jack."

"Shut up Josh! It's all you talk about. Claire this, blonde that. It's wearing, mate. You should take a leaf out of my book, screw 'em and leave 'em. That's my style. Works every time I can tell you."

"But you haven't got a girlfriend."

He raises his beer at me. "Ex-bloody-actly," he grins. "Anyway, based on what you've said Claire's shagging someone else."

"No fucking way." I don't sound particularly convincing to anyone and he doesn't look fooled either.

"Time will tell, mate. Time will tell," says Jack, all sage like.

Unfortunately it does.

A Bit of B&E

Mr Lamb had always found it preferable to be bold in his actions, and never more so than when it came to illegal activities. Breaking was to be avoided when the entering needed to be kept confidential. Ordinarily he would choose a time when 99.9% of the population was guaranteed to be asleep. However, he had little choice in the matter on this occasion. He needed more information and he needed it now.

He walked straight up to the door like he belonged there, picks in hand. The lock was adequate but not much of a barrier to someone who knew what he was doing. Within moments he was in the entrance hall and closing the door gently behind him. He stood in total silence for a full minute, listening intently. He already knew the homeowner did not have a pet and there were no guests staying, but he had stayed alive and at large for so long precisely because he was ultra-cautious.

A motor hummed quietly nearby. It sounded like a fridge or a freezer. Then came a cry and heavy footsteps, but they were from the flat above — probably a parent responding to a child's bad dream. He crept soundlessly in well-worn soft shoes. For a flat the floor space was probably considered quite large but nevertheless it didn't take him much more time to track down the PC than it had to get through the front door. He booted it up, amazed that no password was needed, then waited a minute for the out-of-date operating system to activate before inserting a flash drive. The internal workings of the PC hummed as the worm self-extracted and began slithering its way through the operating system.

Once the worm had infected every part of the computer it shut down. he secreted the flash drive in an inside pocket, crept along the corridor, closed and locked the front door. Within a minute he was in his car and had withdrawn from his latest satisfactory crime on society.

It's Physics Of The Soul

Four pints have been welcomed and taken their leave, more than I would ordinarily drink in a night, never mind an hour. Jack looks at me cross-eyed over his glass. He's tried to shift onto lager, but I neglect to tell him one key fact — this place doesn't sell it. So he's been forced to stick to the cider, a beverage formulated hundreds of years ago to get you off your box fast and hard, and still doing its job exceptionally well today if Jack is anything to go by.

Although alcohol is a fantastic tongue lubricant, too much and it enters the realm of being a verbal laxative. I slur, "Friends, they're like comets."

I can vaguely tell that this is going to be one of those conversations that sound pure genius to the drunks and utter shite to the sober. I'm pretty certain he wants to ask me what the fuck I'm talking about, but he's so pissed he struggles to effectively verbalise. Therefore I have to explain a little more. "So...you're the sun," I point at Jack, confusing him even more, "and like the sun you exert a gravitational pull and, well, that's what you do to people, Jack. Every now and again someone gets close enough and the strength of your personality, charisma or whatever draws the person to you. Some stay in your orbit for a long time, others drift slowly away, never to be seen again. It's what I call *physics of the soul*."

I sit back, grinning broadly, sure Jack cannot fail to be impressed by my immaculate logic. But he still looks utterly nonplussed.

"Time gentlemen please!" interrupts the landlord. "Drink your drinks up now!"

I vaguely recognise that because our discourse has been interrupted my brilliant analogy will more than likely be lost, either because I will forget when I sober up or (more likely) I will *want* to forget when I sober up.

On the other hand it's probably fortunate that we're being turfed out of the pub, as I've reached that dangerous stage when I recognise I'm hammered but the alcohol convinces me that the morning's sufferings will be worth it. I gulp down the last dregs of my beer then stand up, wobble and grab the back of my chair for support.

"Do you want me to get you a taxi?" I slur.

Jack shakes his head. "Schtay at yours," he mumbles. He really is fucked.

I can't be bothered arguing, and actually I'm quite pleased because at this time of night it'll be at least an hour before a taxi will be arsed to turn up and I really should climb into my pit.

"Sure, no problem," I say (although not that distinctly).

As we exit I give a jaunty wave to the landlord, and any other soul still inside who cares to accept it, before stepping outside and immediately regretting it. Pubs seem to exist in a different dimension. It's like stepping across a boundary — inside and outside are utterly different. Inside you're a star, everything makes sense, everything is fun and life is for living. Outside everything is hard — the air, walking, speaking, life in general. It's no wonder some people spend their lives in a perpetual haze.

We weave the short distance to my flat, which of course is challenging (being outside the pub), but we make it eventually because I bravely have my arm outstretched in front of us. I'm a strong man leaning into a powerful headwind. I'm knackered with the effort so I have to crawl up the stairs and to my front door. Every now and again I check behind me to see if the faithful Sherpa Jack is still with me on my escapade. Still on my knees it takes three attempts to get the key in the lock and then we're safe inside again. Jack however suffers a minor carpet burn to the face as he's been getting mutual support from the door.

"Bedroom, bathroom, kitchen." I point to each room in turn as Jack levers himself upright.

"Bed, jusht bed," he pleads.

I point again to where he's going to sleep. He nods broadly in my direction, says goodnight, manages to get to his feet and then staggers into the guest bedroom. He keeps shambling until his shins hit the bed frame, then folds and lands face down on the bed. I'll bet he was unconscious before his injured cheek struck the mattress.

Thirty seconds later I'm in bed myself, stripped butt-naked with my alarm set. All thoughts of Claire, Jack and Konstantin's baffling warning are lost in an alcoholic dream about a mysterious blonde who's begging to give me a blowjob.

Plastered

Claire and Hershey fell out of the restaurant an hour and a half later, rolling drunk. They'd sunk three bottles of wine, most of which had found its way down Claire's throat and borrowed dress (which was going to need a serious dry cleaning and was probably ruined). She had even paid, insisting the bill was on her company because Hershey was the prospective client.

"We didn't even discuss bishinesh," she slurred, swaying like a badly-behaved metronome in the night air.

"Not a problem," Hershey shrugged. He let out a loud belch which drew a raucous burst of laughter from Claire and disgusted sneers from onlookers. "Why don't we do this again?"

"I'd *lub* to," she said, leaning against him for support.

To Hershey's relief a cab chose that moment to draw up at the kerb. He pushed Claire off (who began see-sawing again) and attempted to open the door. After three failed attempts the driver got fed up and popped it open from the inside.

"You take it," Hershey said, stepping to one side gallantly before Claire could invade his personal space again.

"Noooo," Claire wailed, attempting to dislocate Hershey's arm. "Come with me, come with meeeee!"

Hershey shook his head and Claire pouted. "Not fair. You're not very nice!" she whined, sounding like a three-year-old who'd failed to get her own way.

"I'll call you tomorrow to set something up," Hershey promised. He grabbed Claire by the shoulders, turned her around and folded her into the taxi. She sank onto the black plastic seat.

"Oh-kay," she sighed in resignation, weariness overtaking her, shoulders slumping. "Shounds like a plan."

Hershey slammed the door and watched the cab disappear with relief. Immediately he straightened, all pretence of alcoholic torpor dispelled.

"What a thoroughly vacuous woman," he said to himself.

He considered reversing his plan. Clearly Josh was far worse off with Claire than without her. But no, there had to be a reason for Josh's utter humiliation. So, he reminded himself, he would have to go through the whole process even though he knew it would be excruciating.

For once he went home alone, relieved he had only the pleasure of his own company.

I Don't Feel So Good

I wake up with the alarm that last night I'd deliberately set an hour later than normal. Then, it had seemed a great idea but now, in the morning's glare, much less so. I am experiencing the devil's own hangover. My mouth tastes atrocious, like I've drunk canine urine rather than beer; my tongue is as dry and brittle as parchment and my body aches all over. I sit up and then my brain realises where it is and what it's been through and gets all pissy, taking its revenge by pounding my skull like a bastard. Grabbing my head does nothing to hold the reverberations — it fucking hurts. Then my bladder joins in, shrieking at me that it's a distended balloon about to explode and redecorate the walls and ceiling in an unpleasant shade of yellow.

I simply cannot face going into work. The thought of being shaken around for two hours on the never-ending train journey into London is bad enough, but Hershey also hates tardiness and I suspect that after yesterday's antics this will simply be fuel to the flames of rage. I also really must recover in case Claire decides to come home. We've a lot to talk about and looking like death warmed up is hardly going to start the conversation off well.

I can claim a work-at-home day, even though everyone knows this is just a euphemism for doing fuck-all (like writing a book). But it's probably better to claim I'm sick, which is about to be true. Although it's an outside shot, the sympathy might help my case. But before I pick up the phone I need to relieve the seismic pressure on my bladder. I crawl out from under the duvet, slither (sort of) onto the floor, then crawl lethargically down the corridor to the bathroom, like a parched man in a vast desert, my tongue hanging out and panting like a dog. I edge into the tight little space, push the door shut with my foot and lever myself up onto the seat. I tell myself that all over the country pensioners with recent hip replacements must be going through exactly the same process.

As well as being utterly bereft of energy I need to piss like a woman because if I stand up like a real man I'll spray everything and everywhere except the toilet. But I don't care — minimising the pain and post-piss clear up job are my only concerns. Despite the pressure it takes a little time and persistence to get the flow going, but when it does it's a major relief.

After emptying my bladder, which seems to take forever, I grope around in the medicine cabinet for a couple of headache pills. In the end I take four (I assume the manufacturers just say two at a time because they're risk averse). Then I slide back onto the floor (without washing my hands) and resume my asthmatic skulk along the corridor until I reach Jack's door. I get no answer to my pathetic efforts at a knock. Assuming he's still sensibly comatose I push the door open and enter. To my surprise the bed's empty. He's gone. A note scrawled in shaky script in which he thanks me for my 'company' and reminding me of the party on Saturday confirms my suspicions. I put the kettle on and brew a coffee, cafetière, of course, none of that instant shit no matter how rough I feel.

Whilst the coffee grounds are doing their thing I pick up my mobile phone and call Elodie who, you may like to forget, is Hershey's icy French secretary bitch. Amazingly she isn't on strike, like the rest of her countrymen always seem to be, and being unusually efficient she picks up the call on the second ring.

"Hi Elodie, it's Josh. I feel awful and I'm afraid I won't be coming into the office today," I say, thinking I don't have to try too hard to portray how bad I feel.

"Josh who?" Elodie replies.

I hold my temper and say, "Dedman, Josh Dedman."

"Oh yes, *you*. You are *ill* you say?"

"Yes," I croak, "I feel terrible, I think...I think I have the flu or something, I feel sick and my head is pounding."

"It's July," she observes. I can imagine her looking out of the window at the blinding sunlight, "I do not know of *anyone* who has ever had flu when it is ninety degrees in the shade."

"Well now you do."

Elodie snorts, "It is just too much *bière*."

I decide to shut down the conversation as quickly as possible. She's being far too observant for my liking. "Can you tell Hershey, *please*, that I won't be in today?"

"When will you be returning?" she asks in a tone that suggests I perhaps never should and I have a tendency to agree with her.

"I don't know. I may try to struggle in tomorrow."

"Ah *oui*, perhaps the hangover will have worn off by then."

I ignore her. "There's no point infecting everyone. It's not fair and it's not professional."

I swear Elodie laughs but she manages to stifle it. "Well, *whatever,* as you English like to say. I will e-mail you a self-certification form for you to lie on when you fill it in."

"Thanks," I say with mock appreciation and cut the connection, making sure I hear the dialling tone before I say, "you fucking bitch."

I pour myself some coffee, slop in plenty of milk and drink half of it in one, long gulp, relishing the burning sensation as it hits my throat and stomach. Bloody hell I feel awful. I go back to bed but it's challenging crawling down the corridor with a mug full of scalding coffee in one hand, I can tell you.

A Clear Head

Claire popped an eye open when the alarm rang. She'd experienced a heavy, alcohol-induced slumber, the kind where you sleep like a log but awake absolutely knackered. Momentarily she wondered where the hell she was but then recognised enough of her possessions to realise she was in her flat. She racked her brain, but had absolutely no idea how she'd got home. The last thing she could remember was the dessert, but absolutely nothing afterwards.

She needed to figure some things out:

First — attire? She tentatively ran her hands over her body. She felt fabric. She was fully dressed.

Second — alone or with someone? She couldn't detect any heavy breathing, but it was worth clarifying nevertheless. She raised her head slightly and looked around the bedroom. The light was dim but she could make out, with a surprising twinge of disappointment that she was, as she suspected, alone.

"Ah, shit."

She was surprised not to feel guilty at the thought of sleeping with someone other than Josh; in fact she felt a little thrilled by the idea. It had been a long time since she'd last done something really wayward. In fact it had probably been when she'd seduced Josh and that was a *long* time ago.

She lay back for a minute; she had some slack before she needed to get in the shower. She didn't have a hangover as such; she could drink quite heavily and not feel a thing in the morning, and today was no exception. She just felt tired and in need of rehydration and a shower, in that order.

As she lay there she thought about Josh and felt...nothing. Their relationship was like comfortable socks, warm and soothing but the trouble with socks was if you kept them on for too long they became smelly and threadbare. Which was definitely how Claire was beginning to feel. But worn out to the point of being thrown away? Maybe. She wasn't sure.

Then she thought of Hershey and a little fizz rushed through her body. She looked at the clock — the five minutes leeway she always gave herself had been used up. However the residual tingle was still there and she thought she should capitalise on it, why let it go to waste? She had a waterproof vibrator in the bathroom cabinet with a brand new pair of batteries inside. That would prove a great start to the day.

At the same time as Claire was having her second orgasm Serena was sliding into bed unaccompanied. She was absolutely shattered. As predicted it had been one hell of a night. Bloody drunks everywhere, a couple of fights in a bar, loud music, people partying in the hot, still air — it seemed like no one wanted to sleep. She's had to knee one guy in the balls when he'd tried to paw at her tits. He'd immediately forgotten her mammaries and instead cuddled his throbbing bollocks.

James was already long gone, his bed empty and cold. Not that it mattered because they slept in separate rooms, which, according to James, was how the wealthy used to do it right up until the Victorians. As Serena drifted into the edge of sleep she idly wondered who he was shagging. Then she shook her head. No, James was too loyal and far too busy, and besides, she shouldn't judge everyone by her own pitifully low standards.

Duvet Dancing

It's Saturday. Virtually nothing of importance has happened since the last chapter so I'll commit the minimum to paper and avoid boring the arse off you and me:

Wednesday: Totally lost to languishing in my sweaty bed.

Thursday: My hangover all cleared up, I drag myself into work but, as is sometimes the way, I still don't feel particularly great. Probably the few thousand brain cells missing in action, obliterated by alcohol. Once at my desk I e-mail my fabricated self-certified sick note to Elodie and then studiously avoid going upstairs for the rest of the day.

Friday: I was alone in my office without a single visitor. By the time I leave I've heard nothing from Hershey for two days, which is an occurrence as rare as Halley's Comet and frankly the only positive point in what had been a pretty depressing week.

Speaking of being MIA I've seen nothing of Claire either. We spoke, we texted, we met not. So everything I'm bursting to say has to remain unspoken, which is difficult for someone (me) who typically unflinchingly stakes their bleeding heart onto their sleeve, but I tell myself to be strong and hold off blurting my emotions out over the phone. What I have to say has to be face to face.

So to Saturday. My bloody phone bleeps at a ridiculously early hour (10am), tugging me out of a blissful dream that I immediately forget the detail of. There's only the vaguely temperate whisper of the indefinite blonde left, but the sensation is tainted by the frustration of losing her to wakefulness and the jarring acknowledgement that she's only in my mind.

I fumble for my phone, feel the cold, hard casing and crack open an eye at the brightly illuminated screen. For a moment my vision oscillates then finally focuses. The text reads, "Don't forget, party time!!! J." And there's a smiley face...

"Bollocks." I've forgotten all about Jack's bloody gathering.

I drop the phone onto the floor and roll back into the slightly cooler embrace of my duvet. The phone rings, juddering around as it vibrates. I ignore it. It stops ringing, then almost immediately starts again. With a sigh that emanates from the depths of my fading soul I grope around on the floor and appropriate the handset that's jack-knifing around like a landed fish gasping for air. It's fucking Jack. I reluctantly answer, gingerly pressing the phone to my ear like it's a seashell in which I can't quite believe I'll be able to hear the sound of the waves.

"Do you know what fucking time it is?" I grunt. As you can tell I am not in the best of moods.

"Oh don't be so mardy!" Jack chirps brightly.

"Nobody says 'mardy' any more Jack, not in this part of the world anyway."

"I just wanted to remind you of the party later. You're still coming aren't you?" he asks, ignoring my criticism.

"Erm..." I delay. Frankly I'd rather have a kidney removed with a butter knife, but he sounds so keen it's hard for a charitable Englishman (me again!) to say no.

"Don't go pulling out on me now Josh! I need you there, my man!" Jack is like one of those fluffy little lapdogs — an irritating yap, but too endearing to kick in the gonads — so I hesitate a bit more, stupidly giving him an opening he relentlessly pursues. "Come on Josh, what do you say? We'll have a great time!"

In the end it's my bodily needs that win out. Some more sleep is an essential and I figure he won't go away until I agree, so I cave in "Oh, fuck it, why not. I'll be there."

"Yes!" Jack shouts in exultation, as if he's scored the winner in stoppage time at the local derby. "See you at 2pm. Don't be late!"

"Sure," I say, but the line is already disconnected. Jack's probably torn off to slice some more crudités.

I turn my mobile off so no one else (specifically Jack) can interrupt my sleep and banish it to the floor once more. I knot myself into the duvet and again strive to chase the vaporous blonde. But try as I might I can't return to the land of Nod. My limited sex life is a hurdle — as my sperm count rises my Z count drops, proving excess testosterone isn't good for relaxation (however if my theory were strictly true I'd be an insomniac).

When we'd first got together sex was regular and often, as it always is for new couples. But with time, and familiarity, it had dwindled away. Now I have as much chance of having sex with Claire as divining water in Death Valley. Saturday has become shag day but only on the one week in eight when the 'decorators' aren't in and when Claire doesn't have enough reasonable excuses to stop me prising her legs open — i.e. tiredness can't be blamed (because she gets a lie-in in the morning) and nor can having to get up for work the next day.

I remember how she'd attempted to put me off the last Saturday evening we were together — yawning, sneezing, complaining of an upset stomach, the ailments becoming more severe as the evening wore on. Then we'd gone to bed, I'd counted to 100, rolled over and, as she hadn't managed to start snoring, given her a hug. She'd lay there stiff as a log, silently but forcefully communicating her unwillingness to be penetrated.

I'd rolled away and thought about the injustice of it all, as her breathing got heavier and my mood blacker. I'd thought about how sex only happened when she wanted it to, no matter what my urges were. Of course, when Claire was in the mood I was too weak-willed to refuse. Every time she'd blocked me in the past I'd always sworn myself to reject her when the tables were turned. For a moment I'd consider telling her to fuck off, that now I wasn't feeling up for it, but then I'd crumble and accept — I knew Claire wouldn't care if we did it or not and more likely would be pleased to be let off having her vagina splayed. So therefore, I'd reasoned, I might as well achieve some enjoyment.

Perhaps this is why I've begun following girls to work, why the blonde was taking up more of my thoughts. I've never been unfaithful and doubt I ever will, but something is driving my subconscious. I just can't understand quite what it is yet.

Feeling guilty for thinking about other women, I try to call Claire again. It rings once, twice, then goes to voicemail. She's rejected me. Again.

Pendulum

Hershey lived by the 'treat 'em like shit, they'll love it' mantra. So he broke his promise to call Claire the next day. Ordinarily he wouldn't have called her at all; in fact he wouldn't have gone out for dinner with her full stop. However, needs must and after four days he reluctantly tapped out her number on his cell.

"Claire, Hershey," he purred as soon as she answered.

"Hi!" Claire chittered brilliantly. "How are you doing?"

Hershey cringed momentarily and took the phone away from his ear. He heard Claire say hello a couple of times before he steeled himself. Sometimes in life difficult things had to be done to get ahead, although this was right up there in the premier league of shit stuff. He pressed the phone back to his ear and said, "Look, sorry I haven't called, I've had some...stuff to deal with."

"Oh, no problem!" Claire said. "I understand completely. You're forgiven!"

"Great, thanks." He struggled to keep the sarcasm out of his voice. "And sorry I had to leave it to the weekend to call; it's been a crazy time at work."

"I bet!"

"Anyhoo, I wanted to arrange to meet next week, perhaps over lunch? We didn't get chance to discuss business last week."

"That'd be great. Delighted to."

"When suits you?"

"Oh, any day, any time. I'll clear my diary."

"Tuesday?"

"As I said, whenever suits you."

"Tuesday it is then."

"Works for me!"

"Cool, I'll drop you a text to confirm where."

Hershey ended the call, telling himself for the millionth time it would be worth it in the end.

"Oh shit," Claire said to herself.

She was perched on the edge of the sofa, a millimetre away from slipping onto the floor. Tuesday was a terrible day, the worst. But she'd promised to clear her diary and she would move heaven and earth to get Hershey's business and, she hoped, his cock.

Her week had slid from elation after the dinner and her subsequent swagger in the office, to downright depression by Friday when Hershey hadn't called as promised. She was sure her colleagues were giggling behind their hands. Now she would show them and no stupid pre-arranged meetings were going to get in her way.

Her phone rang again. Her heart did a little skip, imagining Hershey had decided instead to invite her out for dinner followed by sex tonight. Her heart sank when she saw it was Josh calling.

She rejected the call, sat back on the sofa. A moment later she laughed long and loud, all the while kicking her feet and windmilling her arms.

Party At The Dean House

It's 2pm. I like to be on time for my appointments. The taxi drops me off at the address Jack had kindly texted me (twice) — an estate which is the rich man's playground in my neck of the woods. Jack's house is a huge sprawl, built relatively recently with the lighthouse in the background and the sea to the fore, which is close enough so that I can hear the sporadic crash of waves at the foot of the chalk cliffs. There's an Aston Martin DB9, my dream car, parked outside a triple (yes, triple) garage. A lovely location but with a price tag to match, I'm sure.

I step through high metal gates which ordinarily block off the oval in and out drive and are bordered by equally high brick walls. There's the throb of muffled but nevertheless still loud music from within the house. I bet the posh neighbours are loving this. I ring the doorbell to the right of a large door painted an austere dark blue. A minute passes with no answer so I press the bell again.

Nothing.

I pull out my mobile and call Jack. His phone rings and rings but there's no answer and no answer machine. Something isn't quite right. Although I can hear music I realise there's none of the accompanying sounds typically generated by a large gathering of people — shrieks of laughter, raised voices, the clink of glasses. Maybe I'm too early or I've the wrong time?

The taxi has long gone meaning no quick exit, so that decides it for me. I walk around the front and then the side of the house and into a much larger landscaped garden dominated by a kidney-shaped swimming pool. In the middle of the water floats a blow-up rubber ring in which Jack slouches in trunks and sunglasses. He's holding a lurid-coloured cocktail which is mobbed with fruit and straws, and he traces a slow circle as the ring leisurely rotates. He looks as miserable as sin. I stand and watch him turn a full 360 degrees but he seems not to notice me.

"Hey Jack," I say.

He raises a lazy hand but says nothing in response.

"Where is everyone?" I ask, looking around. I've been promised flowing alcohol and loose women but I can't see either.

"I told them all to fuck off," Jack says and chugs back a couple of mouthfuls of his cocktail.

"Why?"

"All my friends are twonks," he says and then tosses the half-full glass over his shoulder and into the pool with a 'plunk'. It plummets to the bottom and as it sinks the drink stains the water as if Jaws has bitten some kid's arm off in the depths. "So the party is just you and me, mate."

My utter puzzlement must be plastered all over my face because even though I don't say a word Jack shrugs and says, "Because all my friends are selfish wankers. Except you."

Bloody hell, I think, *if I'm his best friend then he's in real trouble.* And so am I.

"We barely know each other," I try to argue.

He waves me away with a jerk of the wrist. "I know enough about you to believe you're a decent sort," he says, then suddenly cheers up. "Anyway, who needs 'em? Screw 'em, screw 'em all!" He paddles himself to the pool edge (wisely I think, considering the killer fish in its depths). "Come inside for a look around the pad."

Once safely back on dry ground Jack enters the yawning mouth of two big French windows, leaving wet footprints in his wake. Compared to my two-bedroom place it's hugely impressive — a big, well kitted-out kitchen, all pristine stainless steel and marble bedecked with heavy-duty kitchen equipment, a living room the size of a football field occupied by a TV big enough to double up as a goal and other boys' toys, a library packed with books (I want one!), a dining room with a massive table (which looks utterly unused), a study and at least five bedrooms, most of them en-suite. Eventually, after a hike which would have fucked up Michael Palin, we come full circle back to the kitchen.

"Beer?" Jack asks, pulling open the huge, American-style fridge door, then throws me a can without waiting for an answer. Sam Smith's, not the greatest beer in the world, but at least it isn't lager. He's learning, albeit slowly.

Jack, his mood seemingly much improved, pops his own tin, takes a deep draught, belches and laughs.

"So, what now?" I ask.

"Music!" he replies and picks up a remote control. With a flick of a button Friendly Fires are singing in high-definition surround sound from hidden speakers. They're advising we should jump in the pool.

Well, they can have it, I think (killer shark, maimed kid, remember?).

"I love these guys," Jack says, dancing in a circle, beer and remote control raised in prayer as if he's at a festival and toasted on drugs. "They're originals, one of a kind, just like you and me, Josh!"

Well that's a first. I've never been described as a 'one-off' before.

"Ready for another one?" he asks, still spinning and pointing at my barely-touched drink.

"Not for me yet, thanks."

"Girl," he says and grabs another can from the fridge before popping the tab. He downs what was left of the first, tosses the empty into the sink and starts on the second — chain drinking.

"Come on, let's get comfortable," he says, and without waiting for me pads out of the kitchen. I follow him into the expansive living room cum Wembley stadium. He flops down, spilling some beer onto the leather sofa in the process which he either doesn't notice or doesn't care about.

"You know I'm glad it's just you and me," he says. "We'll have a lot more fun. Speaking of fun it's time for another beer."

He leaves the room and I glance around the vastness. Something catches my eye, a gap in an otherwise crowded assembly of photographs on a low table. I cross over and look a bit closer. One photograph is turned face down. Curious I pick it up and turn it over. The picture is in a heavy frame but I barely notice the weight.

"Are you coming for a dip?" Jack shouts from the kitchen.

I can't reply. My mouth won't work. The picture is of the blonde of my dreams...

The Pigeon Takes Flight

Tuesday, and Claire sat at a small table in an unobtrusive bistro impatiently twiddling her thumbs. Tucked away down an alley, the restaurant was secluded but only a few steps away from a busy thoroughfare. The place was a gastronomic oasis. Over the low murmur of the clientele and the business of running a restaurant she could no longer hear the constant sound of commuters or detect the metallic tang of exhaust fumes, only the waft of food from the kitchen. If it tasted half as good as it smelt it would be delicious.

She had arrived early but Hershey, in a repeat of their previous date, was late. She tugged at her suit jacket and smoothed her skirt, feeling badly dressed. This morning she'd rattled through her entire wardrobe to try and find something suitably sexy whilst looking professional, but hadn't come remotely close to the right combination. Just then the bell above the door tinkled and Hershey, *at last*, walked in. He looked around briefly, saw Claire and threaded his way through the closely-set tables mostly filled with business people doing business.

"Sorry," he said as he dragged out a chair and flopped down. He picked up the menu that the waitress had placed on the table ten minutes ago.

"It's becoming a habit," Claire said with a smile. Hershey looked up and a flash of irritation breezed across his face, coming and going in an instant.

Before he could respond the waitress materialised as if from nowhere, pen and pad poised, keen to get them moved on. "Are you ready to order?"

"Chicken Caesar salad for me," Hershey said. "Hold those fishy things."

"Anchovies?" asked the waitress.

"That's 'em."

"Same, please," Claire said.

The waitress evaporated, leaving them with only themselves for company. Claire wanted to get down to the action as well. She bent over to reach for the briefcase she had placed beneath the table, grabbed it, popped it open and extracted a tightly-bound sheaf of paper.

"On the basis of our conversation I've prepared a brief proposal for you to consider," she said and put the document on the table in front of Hershey, almost exactly where the menu had been.

"Okay, thanks." he drawled. He picked up the proposal and flicked through it. He took a couple of minutes to skim through twenty pages whilst Claire held her breath.

"Looks great, let's do it," he said.

She opened her mouth to give her pitch, then abruptly closed it again when she realised Hershey had been positive. "What did you say?" she asked.

"I said yes."

At that moment the waitress delivered their salads and promptly retreated.

"Are you sure? You barely read it." She couldn't quite accept what Hershey was saying, although she was desperate to do so.

"Sure," he shrugged and shovelled a forkful of salad into his mouth and chewed it thoroughly.

"Our fee is on the final page."

"I'm sure that's fine too."

"It's a bit steep."

Hershey shrugged. "I don't care."

"Oh! I don't know what to say."

"How about thank you."

"Thank you!" Claire giggled.

"Are you eating that?" Hershey pointed his fork at her salad.

"Christ I completely forgot." She started eating her lunch, barely registering the taste of the dressing or the crunch of the lettuce. She put her fork down again. "Look, I need to know you really are happy with the rebranding proposal."

"Uh-huh. When you know, you know. You know?" He reached over and squeezed her hand. She felt herself blush. "How about a drink to celebrate?"

Without waiting for her reply Hershey waved the waitress over and ordered champagne. He ate whilst the bottle was being prepared but Claire had completely lost her appetite. She stared around the restaurant as if she wasn't quite sure where she was. The popping of a cork brought her back to her senses.

"Cheers!" Hershey said, toasting her success with a raised glass.

She followed suit and a swallow of the overpriced chilly liquid helped her brain accept her successful negotiation. The alcohol punched her bloodstream like a sledgehammer.

"So, what are you going to do with your bonus? I assume you do get a reward?" Hershey asked.

She nodded. "A new look I think," she said, casting her mind back to her wardrobe difficulties this morning.

"Is that it?"

Before she could think about it Claire blurted, "I could do with a good fuck."

Hershey looked momentarily shocked and then burst out laughing. She joined in, her giggle tinged with relief and disappointment in equal measure. Hershey put his fork down and looked at her thoughtfully but didn't speak. Claire caught his expression.

"What's the matter Hershey, have you changed your mind about the proposal?"

"Yes."

"Oh shit. My boss will fire me for sure now."

"No I'm fine with the rebranding exercise."

"Well, what then..." The penny dropped. "Oh."

"What are you doing Saturday?"

Claire blushed.

Claire was assassinating her plastic. So far she hadn't found the knockout punch — her credit limit was down on the canvas, but not out. Ordinarily shopping was therapeutic, but today it was a celebration of a job well done. Due to the impending contract with the Bank she was set to rise meteorically to the top of P&R's sales table. When she'd called it in Patricia hadn't known whether to be delighted or angry with her so had settled for both — praising Claire for getting the business but then bollocking her for not getting it sooner.

For once she didn't give a flying fuck about Patricia's attitude. She was cast-iron now. The deal was so significant in the PR world that it would bring her to the attention of all the major houses. And with her burgeoning relationship with Hershey, she felt like she had the world at her feet. So she'd reasoned that she might as well spend the money that she would be earning in the future, to maximise the enjoyment of it and catch up on all she'd missed.

Weighed down with bags of clothes and shoes, she swept out of the store. Her old, dowdy garments had gone, left behind on a hook in the changing room. She figured her new look might as well be shown off straight away. It had cost enough.

A glance at her watch told her it was time to get back to work. She marched purposefully to the bus stop, sweeping past other pedestrians with an imperial air, ignoring the noise of the traffic. All around her was serenity. Then she drew up abruptly, the colourful display in the shop window grabbing her attention. She hesitated for half a second then pushed her doubts away and went in.

What felt like hours later she emerged, a little tender of body but transformed of soul. For an interminable period she'd lain on her front, the top half of her body naked except for a bra (she was pleased she'd worn one of her few good ones today) and skirt pulled down to the bum crack, whilst the tattoo artist had punctured her with an inky needle to create the Celtic design at the base of her spine that stretched from hip to hip.

Then she'd sat up and the bra had come off. The next operation was exceptionally faster but significantly more painful. The tattoo artist had swabbed her nipples before piercing them with a bolt. Not feeling in the slightest bit embarrassed Claire had slowly dressed (but not bothered to replace her bra, stuffing it into a bag), paid for the procedures and left the shop.

She'd never done anything remotely so risqué before; her previous low-water mark had been drinking flaming shots at 1am as a student. Claire revelled in the feeling of release. It was addictive, breaking her mother's lifelong rules. Like a gambler on a winning streak or a drug user having the high of their life, she had a vague thought that it might all end in tears, but as soon as the doubt rode up in her mind she pushed it away with a shrug. Now she was on the up she believed failure was something that happened to others — well, from now on at least. She couldn't wait for her next fix and, after only a couple of minutes of tender walking, she found it.

Claire dumped her bags on the pavement and cupped her tiny breasts in her palms. She wondered if Hershey would pay for the surgical enhancement or whether she needed another loan...

"You're late!" Patricia started shouting before she clapped eyes on Claire, pre-warned by one of her office lackeys that the errant employee was returning from an extended lunch break. "Where..."

Patricia stopped mid-rant, staring in open-mouthed shock at Claire's new style, which from top to bottom was decidedly sluttier than the previous bookworm look — knee-length boots, a very short skirt and an equally short shirt which revealed plenty of Claire's flat stomach, but ,despite it having a couple of buttons undone, very little of her flat chest.

"Celebrating," Claire replied before Patricia could get her jaws half way closed. She put the Bank proposal in front of her boss and walked out, giving Patricia one last shock as she goggled at Claire's new tramp stamp.

Lucked Out

I don't know why but I haven't said anything to Jack about the photo in his house. Maybe it's because I need something soft to shroud myself in; everything else in my life is so spiky and harsh.

Work is awful; Hershey is worrying me greatly by being nice all the time and *smiling*. My relationship with Claire is nonexistent. How many times have I tried to contact her and failed? I've lost count. I've no other friends locally. My work colleagues are all twats and I live eighty-plus miles from where I work, which isn't exactly conducive to the male bonding that results from regular nights out on the piss. I did that once, when first at the Bank, and it was a fucking disaster (and no, I'm not going to tell you the story because it's too embarrassing). In comparison Jack has a gradual degrading effect like a steady, ongoing dose of radiation. He wears you down into liking him and he's as mentally challenging as a cuddly toy.

Each morning on the train I search for the platinum blonde. She's invading my days as well as my dreams. She's become my wank fantasy in the shower (look, there's no shagging going on in my tenuous relationship so I have to find some way of sorting myself out as Claire isn't willing). She even disrupts my random walk to work each morning. A nice arse and tits aren't a sufficient qualifier any more — they have to be *her* arse and *her* tits.

Jack and I are talking over a beer in the pub.

"We can easily find her," he says, ever the optimist.

"How, for fuck's sake?" I respond, ever the pessimist.

He tells me...

Pub crawl to the local hotspots.

She's a cute girl, not likely to have kids so she'll be out on the razz on a weekend like everyone else. At some point, after enough drinking, we'll find her, he assures me.

He says, "And if not we'll be getting drunk in the process. Everyone's a winner!"

I'm not convinced but it beats staying in on my Jack Jones like a sad bastard. Again.

"Okay, fuck it. Why not," I say.

So a couple of days later we're in Ramsgate, walking along the harbour, a pleasant stretch of bars overlooking an array of yachts and working boats that mask the more shitty interior of the town. We start at the far end (at a bar run by Eastern Europeans and selling Belgian beers — figure that) and work our way through the pubs, cafes, wine bars and finally to a rowdy watering hole-cum-nightclub that has the balls to get away with charging for entry. By the end of the evening I'm fifty quid down with a spinning head and damaged auditory sensors but no blonde.

"Well that was fucking useless," I complain to Jack in the cab.

"No it wasn't, we had a *great* time!"

"You might have done, I didn't."

"Where you go?" the taxi driver asks.

"Yours first?" Jack offers.

"Don't be stupid," I reply. "Yours is on the way to mine."

"True," Jack replies, but doesn't look happy about it. I'm too pissed to care.

We drive in silence the rest of the way until we near Jack's place. "Drop me off here," he says to the taxi driver. "No point going into the estate."

He gets out of the car then leans in through the door. "Same again next week?"

"Sure," I shrug.

Jack slams the door and the taxi pulls away. I look back through the rear window. He's just standing there, watching me disappear into the distance.

The Pigeon Takes It

"Fucking hell, that was good," Claire gasped as she slid off Hershey and onto the wrinkled bed sheets next to him. Covered in sweat, she panted heavily. After riding him like he was a Grand National winner and achieving three orgasms (a first) Hershey had finally grunted, spasmed and flopped back. Claire had assumed he'd finally climaxed too.

"Fucking A," Hershey agreed in a drowsy voice, an arm flung over his eyes.

Claire lay still staring at the ceiling and let Hershey drift off into his slumber. Let him build up some more energy before the next bout. Once he was snoring steadily she slipped off the bed and padded across the bedroom floor into the en-suite. Once inside she pushed the door to and groped for a light switch. Her fingers found the smooth metal knob and with a flick low-wattage bulbs behind the mirror guttered on, emitting a low hum. Claire stared at her reflection, knowing she was seeing her true self for the first time in her life. She twisted one hip to the mirror, then the other, before turning around and looking over her shoulder at her new tattoo. One bottom cheek was still red where Hershey had slapped it.

She leant her hands on the sink and stared deep into her eyes, trying to look within herself. Behind her was a bathroom cabinet with its own mirror and she could see a multitude of Claire's stretching out through infinity, each one a bit smaller and a little further away than the last. Different Claire's, different lives. But which one was she? She reasoned that sometimes we know ourselves least of all.

An hour ago when Claire had propositioned Hershey she'd been fully aware she was crossing a line from which there would be no return. The tattoo and the piercings were just incidentals. They could be removed or hidden away. But sharing her body with someone else was entirely different. It was a two-way thing. She was letting Josh go and accepting Hershey into her life instead. Now they'd had sex she knew she would be with him for a long time. Claire was the committing sort and she believed Hershey was too.

Handy Bendy Claire, that was her now. Your resident friendly fuck-buddy, Hershey. She grinned and nodded. Instantly the reflections all grinned and nodded back, all of her sisters agreeing with and supporting her on the path she was now committed to taking. She clicked off the light and returned to Hershey.

She needn't have bothered being stealthy. Hershey was wide awake and sitting up in bed, the wall lamp beside him bathing him in a pale, tungsten hue. He watched her as she walked across the room. Claire liked to think his appraisal was appreciative.

"What the fuck are those?" Hershey asked as she slid under the covers.

"Nipples."

"I know that! I meant those stupid lumps of metal you've had shoved through them."

"They're called nipple *studs*, Hershey."

"Well I don't like 'em."

Claire surprised herself by bristling. "Who cares what you think? They're my bloody tits."

"Which, I'll remind you, I have to suck. I got a fucking shock when one of them touched my filling."

Ah." Now she knew what had generated Hershey's yelp earlier.

"I've been thinking of having some more work done to them," Claire said. Hershey raised a cautious eyebrow, not really wanting to know. "Would you like these a bit bigger?" Claire cupped her tits as she asked the question.

"Hell, yeah. To my mind any fella not to be interested in big tits is a fucking queer."

"It only costs about ten grand."

The statement hung in the air between them like a bad smell.

"Are you asking me to pay for a boob job?" he asked.

She shrugged. "Maybe."

Hershey burst out laughing. "You've some balls!"

"I thought you'd know by now I am sorely deprived in the testicle department."

Hershey laughed again.

"Did you see my other addition?" Claire said. Hershey looked puzzled so Claire got out from under the covers and turned her back to him, revealing the tattoo. Hershey wiped the grimace off his face as Claire looked over her shoulder.

"Sweet," he said, nodding.

"Do you like it?"

"Oh yeah," he lied.

"Why don't you get a good look at it whilst you fuck me again," Claire said, dropping onto all fours and pushing her backside out towards him.

Hershey turned out the light.

Bailout

It's Monday and we're in one of the many conference rooms usually reserved for meetings with teams of clients or auditors. It's a big airy space with windows on two sides facing the city and a large, curvy table in the exact centre. The manufacturers claim the irregular design is more inclusive than the standard rectangle, which creates distance, but less confrontational than the circle where everyone faces each other. I think it's total bollocks. A table is a table — you sit, you talk. The only design involved is the deliberate engineering of a price increase on what will always be a piece of fake wood with a several shiny metal legs.

Seated beside me at the organ slab are Hershey, a tranche of suits and Liam. Although he's in HR the Bank believes in wide induction programmes so staff understand every facet of the business. The point of today's discussion is a proposed investment. (No need to bore you with the details, it adds nothing to the narrative.) It's being delivered by some nameless new guy I've never met before. I just hope one of his colleagues has explained Hershey's childish idiosyncrasies or there'll be trouble ahead.

Hershey is already utterly uninterested and makes no effort to hide it, spending more time on his flashy phone and picking his teeth than looking at the projection screen. That and smiling broadly at me. It's utterly rude, but the presenter is just bending over and taking the insult straight up the arse. This is what I hate most. Since the dawn of man there have been twats in the world and there will continue to be even when the sun burns out in several billions of years, but it doesn't mean you have to accept it when someone treats you like shit.

After about fifteen minutes Hershey exceeds his boredom threshold and makes it entirely obvious. First he drops his phone onto the table from about a foot high. It makes a heavy clunk that carries to every corner of the room. Next he spins around in his chair, first one way, then the other. The presenter carries on regardless, a hint of pink on his cheeks. Hershey stops spinning, stares pointedly at the guy, listens to the monotone for another half-minute and plays the final card. He leans over the right side of his chair and mimes pulling a lever.

Oh shit, I think. Clearly the new guy has no idea what was going on.

Neither does Liam, who looks at me in puzzlement. I shake my head at him before he can speak; there's no point in getting involved. Unfortunately we've just got to let it happen. Despite it all the presenter continues when really the best advice would be to shut the fuck up. So Hershey leans over and again mimes the lever yank again, albeit with much more gusto and the inclusion of audio — a whistling sound and explosion. *Finally* the presenter stops mid-flow and just stares at Hershey open-mouthed.

"I presume you're new here?" Hershey asks the unfortunate bastard. He nods in mute reply. "Well, so you know, that was me pulling the ejector seat."

The presenter still looks dumbfounded. He glances around looking for support and gets none. Most people in the room have experience of the ejector seat either first or secondhand. It was an infamous technique of the insensitive man.

Hershey pulls the metaphorical lever one more time and jerks up as if blasted from his chair, eyes already on the screen of his mobile and apparently checking e-mail. Oh, the curse of importance. After a couple of stabs at the keypad he looks up and meets the presenter's wide eyes.

"So you know for next time, just to help you out, the ejector seat means I've had enough and I'm leaving the room. Just don't let it get that far in future. Lunchtime!" he says, then wafts out of the room.

The door clicks shut behind him, a small sound that is very loud in the deathly silent conference room. Liam looks sideways at me with a raised eyebrow. I shrug to say, *I know, he's a twat, but what can you do?*

"I guess that's it then guys," I verbalise.

Silently the suits stand and file out the door. I take pity on the presenter who's sitting still and statue-like, staring at nothing. A Trafalgar Square pigeon shitting on his head wouldn't look out of place. I clap the guy on his shoulder (still no idea what his name is) and exit myself.

In the corridor Liam is leaning against the wall waiting for me. He looks bemused. "What was all that about?" he asks, pushing off and falling into step alongside me.

"As you're an HR Gestapo bastard, I really don't think I should be answering that question."

"My lips are sealed and I'm not a bastard. So tell all."

I know I shouldn't reveal my true thoughts about Hershey, but I can't help myself. I'm tired of him, tired of the Bank and tired of my culpability in its ridiculous and false culture, so I force my political doubts to one side.

"Just Hershey getting bored and wanting to be somewhere else," I reply, shrugging. "He's pretty much untouchable. The Old Man let's him do what he wants and Hershey lets everyone else know it, so he can be as big an arsehole as he likes and no one says anything."

"Does he do it often?"

"Less so these days. Anyone in the know just doesn't bother to invite him to meetings, which is pretty much Hershey's aim anyway."

"So by being irritating he gets what he wants," Liam says. It's not a question.

"I guess so," I reply, "but frankly it suits everyone. We don't see Oz, he doesn't see us. It's best that way."

We walk for a few yards in silence. I nod at a few people I vaguely know even though they're all twats. I put anyone who works for the Bank in that category.

"Do you like Valentine?" Liam asks.

"Like him?" I'm incredulous. "How can *anyone* like him? Even his mother has to hate his guts."

"Okay, different question. Do you respect him?"

Now that's really not much of a question either. He's thinking of the old adage, that you don't have to like someone to be able to respect them and therefore work with them.

"No, absolutely not. He's talentless, work-shy and openly steals everyone else's ideas. I doubt he's ever had an original thought in his life."

As we reach my office Liam asks, "So how has he managed to rise so far?"

I can only laugh. "How does anyone get on in life? On the coattails of others. In this case Culpepper, so the rumour goes. I've always found the Chairman insightful, a shit, but not stupid. Hershey must have something on the old man."

Liam seems to think about that one for a moment.

"Why all the questions?" I ask.

Liam shrugs. "New guy wanting to learn the ropes from an old hand?"

I snort in response. "I only do it for caffeine."

Liam's phone chimes. He pulls it out and looks at it. "I've got to go," he says. "Another meeting. Catch you later."

I sit down behind my desk, thinking about Liam's comments for the merest of moments before I mentally shrug and flip open my mobile phone. I hit 'C' for speed dial, wait a few moments whilst it connects, rings and is finally answered.

"What?" Claire asks, her tone so cold it's ice, ice, baby. I groan. Now that white rap, 80s shit will be rolling through my head for the rest of the day.

"Just wanted to see how you are, darling," I mollify.

"As if you fucking care," she replies. I'm shocked to hear the sharp drag of a cigarette, the exhale of smoky breath like a dragon's snort. No, it can't be. Claire's never smoked.

"Of course I care," I say, though not with a lot of conviction. "Where did you stay last night?" I curse myself for asking — it sounds weak because it is.

"With a friend," she says, deliberately non-committal.

"Do you want to meet for lunch?"

She laughs. "No thanks, I'm busy. I've got some exercise booked in."

Exercise? This is getting stranger by the minute, I think.

"I didn't know you'd joined a gym."

Claire laughs, deeply this time like she's just heard the funniest joke ever.

"I've gotta go," she dismisses me.

"Bye," I say to the ether. I drop the phone onto my desk. You know I could swear that I'd heard her giggle coquettishly just as the connection was being cut.

As usual the decisions are made for me and my lunch hour is to be another period spent alone at my desk. I sigh and nudge the mouse to wake up the monitor, consoling myself with the fact that at least I've some important pinball games to play.

Big Brother Is Watching You

Hershey pulled out his phone and saw a text he'd drafted but not sent. Reading it again he was pleased it hadn't gone. He deleted it and tapped out another one.

Mr Lamb entered the office Culpepper had temporarily assigned to him, closed the door and locked it. He left the key inserted, but twisted forty-five degrees so no one else would be able to gain access. He crossed the small, featureless room to the desk. Besides the chair it was the only furniture present. There were no affectations such as personal items or office toys, not even something as functional as a wastebasket. Once seated he selected another, smaller key, unlocked the desk drawer, tugged it open and withdrew a sleek, black laptop. He placed the laptop on the desk, lifted the lid and turned it on.

Whilst the computer was booting up he sat back and thought, ordering and categorising everything he had learned in his mental filing cabinet and looking for the pattern that, irritatingly, still eluded him (a most unusual notion) but which he knew was there. It must be because £20 million pounds hadn't gone missing of its own accord.

After a few moments the screen brightened and a tiny window asked for a password, which he duly entered, a seemingly random mixture of letters and numbers. The laptop chewed momentarily on the data then granted access, little icons popping up on screen like bursting bubbles. Mr Lamb deftly moved the pointer over the software he wanted to use and double-clicked the mouse.

Days ago he had broken into several e-mail accounts — which had proved shockingly easy — and uploaded spyware onto his targets' computers. The programme, once installed, hunkered down as a hidden file and kept watch on everything that happened on the now infected computer. If he so chose Mr Lamb could watch the targets' activities in real time and review their historical activity at his leisure.

There were really only two targets now, but Mr Lamb had always found it paid to hedge his bets. He checked his watch. Lunchtime. Josh was currently playing games. The others were inactive. That was fine; there was some usage history he needed to review anyway and a few secret camera feeds to check too. He got busy. He had always found activity was inextricably linked to luck, and getting a result was ultimately what Culpepper employed him for.

Deciding he just had to work even harder to get the break that Culpepper wanted, Mr Lamb bent to his task.

Claire was seething. She'd spent all morning snapping at everyone and everything in the office. Even the photocopier had received a significant beating. All because a text offering herself had been ignored for twelve hours — how dare he!

Just then her phone beeped and her mood, the most fickle of metronomes, swung to the other extreme as she read the text. Claire liked the blend of hard and soft, thoughtful and shitty in him. The apology was a gentlemanly touch Josh could never be physically or mentally capable of. Now she thought about it, the rude and selfish way Valentine treated her happened to turn her on. What had been really pissing her off only moments ago was now endearing and sexy, something else Josh was unqualified in.

She hit reply then tapped out, "Yours, big boy."

She congratulated herself for purchasing a particularly large tube of lube yesterday, which was currently secreted in her handbag. She hoped there wouldn't be much left by the time their rendezvous was over.

Hershey grinned with delight as he read the response. He wasn't attracted to Claire in the slightest; she was frankly far too cheap. Tacky he didn't mind, but cheap was a big no-no. He needed a piss and strode out of his office, whistling as he walked.

Elodie picked up Hershey's mobile and scrolled through the text messages. She suspected Hershey was up to something but wanted to convince herself he wasn't. The world dropped away from under her feet when she found the exchanges between her boss and Claire.

When Hershey came back in five minutes later Elodie was at her desk stabbing viciously at the keyboard. She turned her most hostile glare on the bastard, fossilising the wink he gave her.

Fils de salaud, she thought.

A Meeting With A Blonde Called Destiny

"I've found her," I say.

"Who?" Jack's voice sounds tinny and stretched over the phone.

"The blonde."

"You're fucking kidding me!" Jack says. He doesn't sound very happy and he doesn't look it either when he reaches the pub half an hour later.

I grin at him like a lunatic. In my hands I hold the local rag which I'd picked up out of sheer boredom (normally it's an immediate entrant to the recycling pile). On page three (yes, I shit you not) is the picture of the girl who is, literally, of my dreams. There's a brief article with black-and-white photo of her beneath and the caption, 'Local hero, Emily Hollowman, who will be awarded a bravery award on Friday.'

"Emily Hollowman," I say. A face and a name. She is real after all.

"Sounds posh," Jack sneers and takes a heavy swallow of his pint.

The article describes how Emily, a Community Support Police Officer, had broken up a particularly nasty fight, rescuing a youth who was being battered senseless, with no regard for her own safety. She'd been injured in the process, but still managed to nick the violent little bastard who'd started the fight (I paraphrase somewhat, but you get my drift). Anyway, the Area Commander had decided to recognise her efforts and, even better, the article told me where her beat was. Broadstairs.

"Get your coat," I tell Jack, ignoring his grimace.

However, this particular nugget of journalistic data doesn't really help my cause as that night, and every fucking night for the rest of the week, we venture out into town looking for CSPO Hollowman. By Saturday I'm feeling fatter (beer and chips) and poorer (ditto) than I had a few days ago. Although alcohol isn't cheap these days this doesn't seem to deter the local lads and lasses from sinking plenty of it. However, following Jack's theory the busiest night of the week should mean the best chance of finding our hero CSPO, so financial and waistline encumbrance is forgotten.

I meet Jack outside the station. As usual he's well dressed but a little showy for my liking. He also reeks of aftershave. We cross the road and enter the first pub. There are a couple of bouncers on the door, squeezed into black trousers, white shirts and black bomber jackets. And yes, they've got shaved heads.

"All right lads?" says one of the thugs as he holds the door open for us. I nod my thanks, not wanting to get a kicking for being rude, but I don't smile, not wanting to get a kicking for being queer.

Once inside I feel fucking ancient. TVs far and wide show the football results from every conceivable country but the commentary is drowned out by a cavalcade of strident voices and shrill laughter. There are fruit machines and cocktails, jugs of beer (on special offer) and chips covered with ketchup. Young guys and younger mobs of girls crowd the bar ordering large rounds of drinks. And this is just the start of the evening; 7pm (the time now) is early. The bright young things typically start at the top of the High Street and as the evening wears on roil tsunami-like on an alcoholic wave through the remaining drinking establishments, pummelling them senseless.

Within five minutes I twice start to shout at Jack, "Let's fuck off home!" But twice I hold my tongue. The lure of Emily Hollowman is all too strong.

We make our way down the High Street — literally, because it's located on a steepish hill that runs down to the cliff edge which has an even steeper (let's call it vertical) drop to the beach and the murky brown English Channel. It's thirsty work, walking a few hundred yards down an incline, so we have to stop at each drinking house. There are three more (although I hear one has closed these days) before we take a tight left turn into Albion Street which runs parallel with said cliff. Albion Street is the alcoholics' Mecca. It's significantly shorter than the High Street, is on the flat and has five pubs with another three in spitting distance. We dive in...

It's nearing kicking-out time and we're swaying at the junction of Albion Street and York Street, surrounded by pubs and people. The air is full of shouts, laughs and the toots on horns of annoyed drivers who are ignored or told to fuck off.

There's the smell of fried food (courtesy of two chippies and a pizza parlour) and fag smoke because lighting-up indoors is banned these days so instead we poison the fresh air outside. Several girls walk past arm in arm, their heels clacking on the pavement. None give Jack or me a glance. Then a larger group of lads tumbles by, laughing and joking with one another and trying, unsuccessfully, to get the girls' attention. If this is a normal Saturday night you can keep it. I'm as miserable as I'm drunk — no Emily.

"I told you it was a waste of time," Jack says. He's been dejected all night and frankly very poor company.

I decide I'm not giving up just yet. We're in the hot spot where three pubs face each other so there are plenty of people around and the highest police presence as a result. The major draw is The Dolphin because it's the last place in town to close its doors (and it's cheap), so if the shit is going to hit the fan anywhere it'll be here. There are coppers in town but they keep a low profile until they can't any longer.

I take the initiative and go inside. Either Jack will stand outside like a twat or he'll follow. I cast a look over my shoulder; he's reluctantly taking the latter course. Depending upon how sensitive you are the Dolphin either has an air of frivolity or a whiff of menace. Personally I feel my hackles rise immediately.

I throw a thumb at the bar and Jack shrugs. We're so pissed one more is a minimal amount of additional damage. Jack glumly sets himself in a relatively clear space — i.e. only five people per square metre of floor — and behind a large barrel cluttered with empty glasses. I squeeze my way to the bar and surprisingly quickly acquire the attention of barmaid (waving a twenty like a flag will do that for you sometimes). She takes my order without expression, although the bloke next to me looks less than pleased with my expediency. She returns with the drinks and snatches the offending note out of my hand, replacing it with one of a much smaller denomination and a few bits of shrapnel before turning away to the next drinker in line. Clutching the two bottles I squeeze my way through the queuing bodies.

"Here you go mate," I say and pass him a beer.

I lift the bottle to my lips and then everything goes dark...

Ouch

Miles away in the capital the two sweaty people had no idea they were being watched by a tiny lens as they fucked each other's brains out.

Claire was already on her second orgasm. She knew she was going to walk like one of those cowboys from Brokeback Mountain for several days. Better than the sex, though, was the fact that, from the look of his apartment, Valentine was clearly loaded and (even better) absolutely in need of a full-time partner to help spend it. She planned to be that person. She pushed back on Hershey with renewed vigour to help persuade him of her value.

Jack couldn't believe how things had changed in a matter of heartbeats. One moment he'd been having a drink, the next Josh was on the floor having been hit by a flying stool — the kind you sit on, not what a nurse asks you to squeeze into a pot. He dropped to his knees and leant over Josh. There was blood everywhere. Over his head a fight got into full swing (literally) but he barely registered it. His one and only friend might be dead! And what had he done to protect him?

Nothing. Jack hated himself.

Then...reprieve. He could see Josh's chest rising and falling as he breathed in, breathed out. Jack almost laughed. He was familiar enough with Josh to know he'd have been pissed off if his life was curtailed by something as mundane as cheap bar furniture.

Men and women in neon green uniforms flooded into the pub, the largest proportion dealing with the mauling punters. Two paramedics came over. One moved Jack gently out the way. He stood up and watched impotently as the pair worked on his friend. Right there and then he swore he would do anything and everything in his power to protect Josh.

He felt a light hand on his shoulder. "You okay?" the blonde CSPO asked him. "Are you hurt?"

"No I'm fine, Em. I'm just worried about Josh."

"He'll be okay," she said. "I've seen worse, much worse."

Jack wasn't sure if that was supposed to make him feel better or not.

"I'd better get back to it," said Emily Hollowman. "Lots of bastards to nick tonight."

"Alright Em, see you later." Jack watched as his sister-in-law threaded her way back through the onlookers, ignoring the admiring looks from some and pig snorts from most.

Hershey suppressed a sigh, glad the thrashing, groaning Claire was on her knees and unable to see the expression of pure boredom on his face as he thrust mechanically away, like a Welshman pleasuring a random sheep. He was secure in the knowledge that he could keep this pace up all day. He was simply going through the motions, metaphorically fucking Josh as well as Claire. Although this was just the start. Now he was ready there was much, much more he would be doing to Josh once he was able to get this mad cow off his cock.

What felt like hours later, but was in fact only sixty, albeit bruising, minutes, he was finally alone. He'd managed to eject Claire, having ejaculated several times. She wasn't satisfied and would clearly have liked to carry on, but Hershey had had enough and made it abundantly clear she was to leave. Fortunately she was keen to please him so, despite a sulky expression plastered on her make-up-smeared face, she'd left, but not without a fight.

"Can't I at least freshen up?" she whined, standing at his front door with knickers in hand.

Hershey was about to tell her to fuck off when the snooty Mrs Howe from next door stepped outside. Before she could catch sight of the bedraggled Claire and her soiled knickers he dragged her back inside.

"Sure, you know where the bathroom is," he said.

"Thanks," she breathed, not realising Hershey was tackling a potential embarrassment, rather than coming to her aid.

After five foot-tapping minutes Claire slid out of the bathroom, looking significantly cleaner, but still as plain as a three-day-old cod. Hershey held open the door.

"Bye again."

"Call me soon?" Claire she asked and leant in for a kiss. Hershey turned his head and accepted the dry peck on his cheek.

"Sure," he lied. With relief he closed the door then leant against it, feeling absolutely shattered, his legs slightly weak.

One surprising outcome was that Hershey momentarily developed a grudging respect for Josh. There must be something about the guy if he could put up with her for as long as he had. Then he squashed the feeling, replacing it with a healthy dose of contempt. Josh was clearly feeble of mind to be still in a relationship with the mad cow. Even getting involved with her proved Josh was an idiot — a revelation he didn't apply to himself, of course, because there was method to his madness.

He flopped down into a large, squashy chair, gathered himself for a moment, then placed a call to his friendly police officer.

"It's me," he said when the call was answered.

"Who's 'me'?" the officer replied cautiously.

"Hershey."

"What the fuck are you doing ringing me on this number?!" The words were hissed, the tone low and muffled, as if a hand was cupped over the phone.

"I need something from you."

"Oh do you?" The response had a concrete overcoat of sarcasm.

"I can keep ringing you or you can talk to me for two minutes and I'll fuck off."

There was a long moment of silence before the officer said, "Hang on a moment." Hershey waited impatiently as his contact moved to another location, outside by the sound of the sudden traffic noise. "Does it have to be now?"

"Yes," said Hershey, "otherwise I wouldn't have called you.

"For fuck's sake."

"Don't forget I have your balls in a sling," Hershey cautioned.

"Don't threaten me."

"I'm merely stating a fact."

"You're a cunt, do you know that?"

"You and me both."

There was the sound of a match striking, a long inhalation and then an exhalation of breath. "What do you want?"

"Some bank details," Hershey said.

"Christ! That won't be easy."

"That's not my problem, is it? Have you got a pen? Because you've got some long numbers to write down and I know what you guys are like when it comes to recalling facts."

The Ward

I look around me. Nope, I don't recognise a thing. The pounding inside my skull doesn't help, neither does the squint. I seem to be in a small white cubicle, although the walls are rippled and uneven. I am reclining, but not entirely flat. Overall I feel quite warm and cosy, despite the pain. Feeling around with my hands I come to the conclusion that I'm in bed. This is confirmed when the wall briefly parts and a nurse enters. For wall, read curtains. I'm in hospital then.

"How are you feeling Mr Dedman?" the nurse asks, a matter-of-fact expression on her no-nonsense face as she looms in closer to look at me. This helps briefly as my world darkens and I don't have to squint quite as much.

"Crap, nurse," I croak.

"It's matron. Take these please. They're painkillers. They'll help with the headache." She hands me a tiny plastic container the size of a thimble with a couple of pills inside, then a glass of water. I tip the thimble up, shaking the tablets into my throat, and follow up with the lukewarm insipid water to send the drugs splashing down into my stomach.

"How do you know I have a headache?"

"Well you've a nasty bump on the back of your skull and we gave you a couple of stitches. In my experience that usually hurts."

"Oh. Makes sense."

She disappears through the curtain, then leans back in a moment later, her floating head seemingly disembodied. "And I forgot to say there's someone here to see you. Two minutes and no more."

"Hi," Jack says sheepishly.

"God, Jack! Are you okay?"

Jack sits down in a chair next to my bed. I try to twist to see him but a pain rockets through my head. "Ouch! Fuck!"

"Yeah, I'm fine," he says, dragging the chair a few feet so I can look at him without moving, but oddly he won't meet my eye. "I'm glad you're alright."

"What happened to me?" I ask.

"Someone hit you with a stool."

"Why?"

"Don't you remember?"

"I can't recall a fucking thing from the point we walked into the pub."

"Oh! That's good."

"Is it?"

"Sorry." He looks flustered. "I didn't mean it that way. Look, I'd better leave you alone or that nurse will be in giving me a hard time."

"She's a matron."

"Well, whatever. I'll see you tomorrow. They tell me you'll just be kept in overnight for observation."

"Thanks for coming in Jack," I say, meaning it. "You're a real friend."

"Really, it's nothing," he says, all sheepish again. A blush develops on his cheeks, then he's gone, the curtains rustling in protest as he slides out between them.

I lie back, somewhat confused by Jack's behaviour. However, I feel like shit so perhaps he's really fine and it's just me. I give up thinking; it's making my head hurt more. Then I imagine I hear a voice I recognise. A pause and I hear it again. I need to confirm my suspicions. At a glacial rate a geriatric would be proud of I pull the sheets back and swing my legs around. Straightening my back points my feet to the floor, a quick shuffle of my bum and I slide down. My feet meet the cold, clammy lino floor and I'm out of bed. I have a pounding headache but I ignore it. I shuffle the two feet to the curtain and poke my head through. I can see Jack, or his back at least. He's leaving the ward with a police officer, not a real one though — one of those community support officers, marked out by the blue on her hat and uniform. I can't see much of her, other than a slim build. Her face is turned away and her hair is tucked into her hat.

Then they're out of the door and out of sight. I follow, shuffling across the ward and eventually into the corridor. I look in both directions, but no Jack and no pretend police officer. As I return to my bed I'm even more confused. I'm convinced I recognise the officer's profile.

I should do. I dream about her enough, my blonde.

Parklife

Hershey's tame police officer rang him back twenty-four hours later. Hershey was in a phone box miles away from the Bank in a location he'd never ordinarily be seen dead in (although murder was a distinct possibility around here). He looked nervously through the scratched plastic panes at the pedestrians outside. They weren't too bad, just sullen guys, blacks and whites alike, most of them with hoods over their faces walking aimlessly. It was the groups standing around that he didn't like, on corners, outside shops, on bikes, in beaten-up cars. They eyed everyone in the vicinity, as if they were a pack of hyenas weighing up potential victims. He hoped like fuck that the taxi driver wouldn't get spooked and clear off because then he'd really be in the shit.

"I've gone to some serious lengths to get this for you, Valentine," the officer said. "I hope you appreciate that."

"And you're being well paid for it. That's all the appreciation you need as far as I'm concerned."

"Not well enough. This'll be the last time I help you out. There's a big clampdown on corruption going on around here."

"Fucking cut it out," Hershey said, his tone cold and heavy. "You leave the arrangement when I say so."

"No, fuck you, Valentine. I have as much on you as you have on me."

"But I'm wealthier."

"And I'm the law."

"Yes but for how long after they find out about your extracurricular activities? E-mail the details to me."

There was a sigh and a long pause. Eventually the officer said, "Thirty seconds and you'll have it."

"Good."

"*Never* call me again," the officer said and disconnected the call. Hershey didn't believe him; he'd be back on the phone looking for work once money got tight.

He waited impatiently for the allotted time. A quick in-and-out was all he wanted, no more. Just to create a trail of breadcrumbs for the law to follow. Speaking of breadcrumbs, a dirty pigeon flew down onto the pavement outside the phone box and fixed him with a beady eye. There were those that said feeding the pigeons gave them an enormous sense of well-being. Bollocks, Hershey thought, and banged on the door to chase the lice-ridden rat with wings away.

True to the officer's word the e-mail arrived, actually slightly ahead of schedule. Hershey smiled to himself. It was all coming together. The taxi driver tooted his horn and waved at him to get a move on. Hershey held up his fingers to signal two minutes then placed another call, this time to Clive, his pet IT geek.

"It's me," Hershey said. "I need to you to do something for me fast."

"Who's this?"

"For fuck's sake, let's not go through this again. I haven't the time."

"I need your codeword. You could be anyone."

Hershey sighed. "Tinkerbell. Satisfied?"

"Go ahead, I'm ready."

"I need you to transfer £20 million pounds between two accounts. Got a pen?"

"Speak."

Hershey rolled his eyes then told Clive the bank account numbers and sort codes.

"And I need you to make the transfer very fucking obvious, so obvious the biggest moron could trip over it. And I need It done quickly."

"Which costs more money."

"Fucking hell, I'm already paying you well."

"I'll say goodbye then..."

The taxi driver honked his horn again, one long beep that lasted several seconds. Hershey felt he wouldn't be waiting for much longer.

"Oh all right," he agreed in a rush. "I'll pay you 25% more than last time."

"50% or nothing."

The horn blew again, a couple of toots. The locals were looking interested too; a couple of hoodies on BMXs rode towards the phone box then began to trace lazy circles.

"50% extra it is! I'll contact you again to move the money into another account but that transaction needs to be very discrete. No one should be able to trace where the money goes. Okay?"

"Okay."

"So move the money in now, big and obvious. Then move the money back out again all clandestine when I tell you, get it?"

"I said *okay*."

"Good, just don't fuck it up!" he snarled. He slammed the phone down then ran to get the taxi, which was just beginning to pull away from kerb. "Stop, you bastard!"

The taxi jerked to a halt. He pulled open the door and jumped in. The BMX riders cruised up alongside the car and leered into the window.

"And I'll be charging you extra for callin' me a bastard," the driver told him as he pulled away with a jerk.

Clive disconnected the call. His heart was thrashing around in his ribcage. He wasn't anywhere near as cool as he'd made out on the phone. His management book had told him to strike hard bargains. The writer had said it would be challenging. He'd lied — it was worse. But he'd stuck it out and earned half as much again as last time, which had already been pretty amazing pay for someone like him.

He nudged the mouse and the computer screen immediately came to life. Out of curiosity he looked up the destination account (he already knew the source). A couple of keystrokes later and his hands froze over the keyboard. The computer screen had four words on it.

Account Holder: Josh Dedman.

"Oh shit," Clive whispered.

Hershey sat back in the taxi and closed his eyes for a moment, ignoring the less than smooth driving of his still angry charge. He hadn't really needed the money. He was already wealthy, not having children did that for you, and being a banker helped, of course. His industry generated a pot of gold at the end of every statement. Even better, as a foreign national he managed to avoid most if not all of the tax that the average fool paid to the British government. No, appropriating the money had never been about financial reward, always about emotional recompense. His mind drifted back to when it had all begun...

"Would you like a drink, Hershey," Culpepper had said, holding up a crystal decanter. An excellent malt whisky (*not* Scotch) would be contained within its transparent walls, Hershey knew.

"Sure, thanks," he said. He hated whisky, but politics demanded he suppress his palette in favour of his boss's.

Culpepper added a small amount of mineral water (*not* ice) to 'reveal the flavours in all their glory,' as the Chairman, a high priest of whisky religion, always intoned, then handed the glass over. Hershey took an apparently appreciative sip, held back the reflexive gag, and lied. "Fantastic stuff."

Culpepper frowned at his malt being called 'stuff' and Hershey panicked for a moment until the cloud passed from the Chairman's face when he took a sip of his own drink. They were sitting on huge leather sofas that comprised the lounge end of Culpepper's voluminous office on the top floor, all of it, of the Bank. It was an astonishing spread of real estate, with private dining room, associated kitchens and top chef, wine 'cellar', golf driving range and even a bedroom where Culpepper could stay when working late (in the metaphorical sense, Hershey suspected). It was an empire, a reflection of Culpepper's influence that few were privileged to see, even Hershey. He wondered what the fuck was going on.

"I assume you're wondering what the fuck is going on, Hershey," Culpepper said, displaying scarily accurate intuition.

"No," he lied, attempting to look nonchalant, and took another sip of the amber piss.

"It's a bit delicate, I'm afraid," Culpepper said, surprising Hershey as the Chairman wasn't one to prevaricate. He liked his confrontations to be a sharp stab in the chest so he could watch the pain on the other person's face. "You know you're my numero uno? My guy?" Hershey winced at the very English Culpepper attempting an Americanism. It was like watching a snake trying to swallow a hedgehog. Next it would be a slap on the back or a punch on the arm.

"Sure I do, sir."

"Great. And you still will be after the changes."

"Changes?" Hershey didn't like the sound of this.

"Yes, I'm getting old, slowing down; I can't do as much as I used to be able to." Culpepper smiled disarmingly.

"I don't believe it, sir!"

"Nice of you to say, Hershey, but I am. So my youngest son, Jacob, will be joining the business soon as my left-hand man."

Hershey froze, stunned. Culpepper's children had previously shown absolutely no interest in pursuing the family trade.

"Meaning?" Hershey asked, knowing already what the answer was.

"Jacob will one day fill my shoes, but you'll still be the numero uno."

Yes, thought Hershey, *Second fiddle to a snot-nosed kid rather than an incompetent old bum*. He'd always believed — no, *been told* — he would inherit the earth once Culpepper left it.

"Why, Ian? Why not me?" he couldn't help but ask.

Culpepper sighed, drained his glass and refilled it, a frown revealing the many wrinkles across his face. He sighed again.

"You realise," he said heavily, "that the decision wasn't mine. The Board insisted."

"Insisted on what?"

"That the Bank maintains an English image. So an Englishman should run the business."

"For fuck's sake Ian, what century are we living in?" Hershey asked, seeing straight away he'd made a big mistake. Culpepper's face flushed.

"It's not the *future* that's important, Valentine, it's the *past*! Too often in this fucking country we bury our heritage for the sake of some incomer, some illegal immigrant. Well not here. Here we draw the line."

"Incomer? Immigrant?" Hershey repeated.

"Oh, you know what I fucking mean!" Culpepper barked, draining his glass and refilling it for a third time. He sighed, visibly calming himself and lowering his voice. "Look Hershey, it's nothing to do with you personally, it's the brand. Most of our major investors are traditionalists. They wouldn't be pleased with your appointment."

"So I stay as vice-captain?"

"In reality you'll be captain, following your analogy, in all but name. Jacob is a nice lad but he's fucking clueless when it comes to the business of investment."

Which just makes the decision all the worse, Hershey thought. It simply wasn't good enough for him to be running things behind the scenes. He wanted to be *out there*. Everyone needed to *know* he was The Man. None of this bollocks that he often heard, that it's the job that you do that's important, not the title that you have. That was total horseshit spouted by unambitious failures. But he knew he would never change Culpepper's mind. The Board had nothing to do with it, they did what he told them.

"Okay, sir, your call," Hershey capitulated.

Culpepper grinned, sounding surprised. "You're sure you're okay with this?"

"Sure I'm sure!" Hershey grinned in reply.

"Good man!"

As Hershey left Culpepper's suite something hardened inside him. He thought of the phrase that goes, 'The more money you earn, the less shit you eat.' Well, he was paid plenty of money, but he was still forced to eat plenty of shit, and now he was being fed even more by Culpepper.

He wasn't going to take this lying down. He was going to shovel some shit of his own. Something had to be done. Something that would hit at the very heart of the Bank.

Hershey came back to the present as the taxi pulled up outside the Bank. Suddenly he was in a good mood and he didn't mind at all that the driver stayed true to his word and piled on an extra and exorbitant charge. He tapped his foot impatiently as the lift transported him up to his office. He blanked Elodie and, once inside his space, began printing off sheets of paper and adding them to a file he kept locked in his drawer. He ignored Elodie again as he breezed out. He didn't bother to wait for the lift but ran up the single flight of stairs and entered Culpepper's lair without knocking. He placed the file on the Chairman's desk.

"What the fuck's this?" Culpepper demanded.

"Evidence," Hershey said in a solemn undertaker's tone.

"Of what?"

"Embezzlement by one of our key employees."

"I don't understand, Hershey."

"It's all in there, Ian. I'm really sorry to bring you this, but I had to."

Culpepper just stared blankly at him, a look of utter confusion stitched on his features.

"Take a look if you don't believe me. It's all in there."

"Oh, I believe you think there's something in there, but the auditors didn't find a thing. All the accounts stack up, so whatever you have, it's meaningless bullshit."

"But Ian!" Hershey protested.

"Shut the fuck up. I'm not sure what game you're trying to play here but I'm fucking wise to it and I don't like it. Get the hell out of my office! I'll decide what to do with you later."

When the door closed on Hershey's back the Chairman picked up the phone. "Get up here now," he said, then turned his attention to the file.

By the time Mr Lamb arrived Culpepper had the gist of the contents. He handed it over and said, "What do you think of that."

Mr Lamb read it through. "It's very convenient," he said.

"Precisely my thought."

Mr Lamb waited for Culpepper, who was a thinker, preferring to crunch data before making a decision. "Suggestions?" he eventually asked.

"I think you've got to cut Dedman loose, make it look like you're taking action. That you've caught the culprit and sorted it out."

Culpepper nodded. "You're right. Burn him."

The Chairman plucked the phone out of its cradle and called Human Resources. "Get rid of Josh Dedman," he ordered. He listened for a moment. "I don't give a shit about how, or what the implications are. We've got deep pockets. Just get rid of the little bastard. Immediately."

He put the phone down and let out a deep breath. "You know, we could even get more clients out of this if we do it right."

Mr Lamb, not one for emotional responses, felt a shiver down his spine.

"Now all we've got to do is decide what to do with Valentine," Culpepper said.

"At least we know who stole the money."

"Yes, but you'd better get going if you're going to close all this out personally."

There's A Dedman Walking

It's all a complete surprise and really doesn't do much for my cranium. My head is sore and the stitches itch like a bitch, but I am a dedicated employee so Hi-Ho, to work I go. But not for long, because two security guards hustle into my office. One unplugs my laptop. He's a little confused when my screen doesn't automatically shut down, clearly unfamiliar with the fact that they run off a battery.

"Blackberry and pass key," the other guard demands, ignoring his colleague's difficulties.

I take my Blackberry out of my pocket and my pass key from around my neck and drop them on the desk an inch short of the guard's outstretched hand, like a suspended cop reluctantly handing over his gun and badge. I'm familiar with this practice as I've seen it several times before. One ingredient in this melange, a representative from HR, is all that's missing.

"Ah, here you are," I say as balance is restored. "I'm glad it's you."

"Sorry Josh," Liam apologises and holds up his hands in apology. "Not my choice and I have to say I don't agree with it."

"It never is."

Liam turns to the security guards. "I'll take it from here."

The guards give me a glare, one of them even doing the 'I'll be watching you' signal, pointing two fingers from his eyes to me then back again, several times, before leaving.

Twat, I think.

A moment later I exit my office for the last time to walk through the open plan with Liam at my side. News evidently has this ability to break one of Einstein's Laws, because it's travelled faster than the speed of light. The room is silent. Everyone is watching me do the walk of shame, some on their feet, openly staring, others a little more respectful and guiltily peeking over the top of their desk partitions. It's like someone has pressed pause during a DVD and halted everyone mid-action — phones to ears, mouths open, fingers poised over keyboards. All it needs is for someone to say "We got a dead man walking here" for the scene to be complete.

Liam presses the lift button. It takes an age to arrive and all the time I can feel their eyes boring into my back. Then there's a ping, the lift doors slowly slide open and I step in. I turn so I face Liam, but don't see anything of the open plan other than in my peripheral vision. As the doors close the hubbub of the office starts up again. Not one of my now ex-colleagues has said goodbye.

"You need to watch out for yourself," Liam says in a low tone. He has to repeat himself as the first time his words don't register. He's looking straight at the doors, not at me.

"I know, the employment market's a bitch right now."

"No," he says, shaking his head. "I don't mean that." He turns to look at me. "They're planning to do you for embezzlement. You're not being fired; you're being suspended whilst an investigation is carried out."

"Embezzlement?" I can't believe my ears. It's not true, surely?

"Yes," Liam says as if reading my thoughts. He hands me an envelope. "It's all in there."

I slide the envelope, unopened, into my jacket pocket. It can wait.

"Take this too." Liam hands me a small square of white card. I glance at it. It's blank except for a mobile telephone number. "In case things get really knotty."

"Thanks." I add the card to the envelope in my jacket pocket. I feel momentarily heavier, the world presses down on my shoulders but it's just the lift drawing to a halt. Once the doors are open wide enough I step out and stalk, head held low, across the reception area and out onto the street. I glance over my shoulder. Liam nods at me from the lift before the doors close on him. Not even the busty receptionist says goodbye.

It's only been ten minutes since the security guards entered my office, and here I am outside the Bank with a small box of valueless possessions, a tender skull and not a clue what to do with myself. I see myself in the reflection of the highly-polished window. I look pathetic, I decide. I lift the box over my head then let gravity take it out of my hands. I turn and start walking away before it hits the ground.

The Next Stage Of The Plan

Hershey heard the rumour within minutes. Although everyone thought he was an asshole, he was an important asshole, so there were plenty of sycophants ready to endow him with information. A quick call to HR confirmed the rumour as fact.

He leant back in his chair, taking a moment to savour the success. After his altercation with the Chairman, he hadn't seen this coming, nevertheless it was a result. His brief self-congratulation over, he dialled.

Claire put the phone down and paused momentarily. Although she was ready she still had to steel herself to take the next step. This was it. This was when she closed the door forever. After a deep breath she picked up the phone again, tapped in a number. It rang twice and was picked up by someone capable of doing the job.

It was time to put the next stage into action. *Balls out*, Hershey thought. He pulled over a pad of paper and scribbled down six names, then added another after a brief pause. He picked up the phone and hit a single button. The speed dial rattled in his ear, rang once and was picked up.

"Hershey," said a deep voice drenched in tobacco fug. "What can I do for you?"

"I'm really sorry to bring you this, sir," he said, "but we have a problem that you should be aware of..."

Five minutes later he disconnected the call, but kept the receiver to his ear as he dialled his IT geek, Clive. Whilst he waited impatiently for the call to be answered he crossed the first name off the list.

"Hello, it's me. Just to let you know I won't be in need of your services any longer." He listened to the protests for a few seconds, got bored and cut the other person off. "No, there's no chance of any further work." He made to put the phone down, the other person still trying to talk him around, then thought better of it and put the receiver back to his ear. "And by the way Clive, you're a sad fucker without a friend in the world. I think you'll die a lonely bastard." He disconnected and put the receiver back in its cradle, a smile on his lips.

He erased the second name.

He stood, crossed over to his drinks cabinet and poured himself two fingers of bourbon into a heavy cut crystal glass. He drank half the fiery auburn liquid. The alcohol seared his throat and landed heavily on his empty stomach. He took the glass back to his desk.

Contact number three was his secretary, Elodie. He told her by e-mail of his impending promotion and that as a result she was no longer his secretary, or anything else for that matter.

Number four was, ironically, only four digits long, an internal call to Culpepper, but he cut the connection before the Chairman could answer it. *Let the Board get hold of Culpepper,* he thought. *More fun that way.*

His phone trilled. He looked at the screen. Elodie. "That was quick," he mumbled and let it ring out.

Hershey jumped to the sixth name on the list because there was some activity number five needed to complete first. The call was answered quickly and efficiently, as would be expected.

"Police, please," he said. "I've a serious crime to report..."

They All Laughed...

I'm still dazed and confused when I get home at an unknown hour.

I'd contemplated going straight home, but I knew there was an hour between trains at that time of day. So I went to a pub instead, any pub, any place that sold alcohol. I staggered on through pint after pint, pub after pub on the way to the train station, which I eventually found myself outside by pure luck.

"Fuck it," I said and belched. "Time to go home."

I fell asleep on the train almost immediately, luckily waking at Ramsgate, the first bit of fortune I'd had that miserable bloody day. Then I wended my way home, via every pub I saw, which fortuitously is relatively limited in number between Buenos Aires and the Old Town. John, the landlord of my local, had to bodily throw me out when I got rowdy and neither of us was pleased about me being unable to pay my tab. He told me if I didn't fuck off I'd be barred, a threat I took pretty seriously, I can tell you.

Somewhere along the route I misplaced my bag. I've no idea whether I left it behind or some opportunistic thieving bastard nicked it. Either way, it'd gone by the time I got back to my flat.

So I'm pretty fucking shitfaced. I do the usual drunk's thing, failing to stab the key into the Yale lock even after lots of practice. Eventually I get there (think monkeys and Shakespeare, blind luck will eventually get you a result) and spill through the door. The carpet is rough against my face, the smell from hundreds of shoes pretty potent. It feels like George Michael is scraping his unwashed stubble on my cheek. I push myself onto my knees, crawl to the stairs and up the three flights to my floor.

From there it's a pretty annoying journey to the door to my flat. Some inconsiderate bastard has haphazardly dumped bags of rubbish along the hallway. Out of the black plastic sacks spill a chaotic variety of possessions, mostly clothes, DVDs, CDs, useless crap like that. Maybe this is a charity collection. I don't know and don't care; I just don't like it being in my fucking way. I reach my door and sit back on my haunches, my bleary eyes level with the lock, a five-lever this time, not a crappy Yale. So theoretically more straightforward to get the key into? No, my friend. I'm just as shit at hitting the target, but after a few attempts (monkeys part deux) the key enters the hole, turns and...fuck all. The lock won't budge. I try turning it both ways several times. Nothing. I only have the two keys on the ring so it's not a case of mistaken entry.

Then I notice the envelope with my name on impaled by a brightly-coloured drawing pin to the door. I pull it down, tearing a thin line in the envelope in the process. There are three tears, so someone else has been reading my mail. The envelope isn't sealed, merely folded in on itself, so even a drunk bastard like me can understand its contents. On the cheap paper inside is typed a short statement:

Dear Mr Dedman,
We have been instructed by the owner of this flat, Miss Claire Pigeon, to evict you forthwith for alleged non-payment of rent. As several notices have been served and ignored and threats made against Miss Pigeon we have been forced to enter, remove your belongings and change the lock. Should you require any further information please contact me.

There followed a mobile telephone number, but no name. I read the note several times, struggling to take it in and sobering up extremely quickly. My interpretation is that I've been thrown out of my flat, but what notices are they referring to? I don't remember being served anything. I certainly can't recall threatening Claire, either. I dial the number on the paper but it goes straight through to the standard service provider voicemail message. I disconnect. Then I call Claire. It rings twice then she answers, but there's complete silence on the other end.

"Claire?" I say. No response. "Claire, I know you're there. What the fuck's all this about?"

Silence, but I think I can hear breathing. Then a giggle, cut off abruptly as the call is disconnected.

"Fuck!" I redial but it goes straight into voicemail, same on the third and fourth attempts.

Then my phone beeps to deliver a text message that reads, "Consider yourself dumped you miserable shit. C. XXX (not)."

I look up and down the corridor at the rubbish sacks containing what I now know is what's left of my possessions.

It's clear now some bastard has been rifling through them. God knows what's been stolen, but I really don't give a fuck because it means nothing compared to what I've already lost.

All I want is my shitty little life back. I feel like I'm in a very small boat in rough seas, I've no idea what stability means anymore and there's no sight of land. Compared to where I am now my inconsequential job, arsehole boss and meaningless relationship are infinitely better.

I call a taxi and wait outside for it. I think it starts to drizzle, but I'm not really sure. A car draws up. I stumble inside, mumble Jack's address and sit back on the sticky seat.

I don't see any of the grey houses through the rain-streaked window. What rolls around in my mind, back and forth, is the sound of Claire's giggle. It sounded...vindictive. And very, very final.

The Only Way Is Up

Hershey dialled the number stored in the phone's memory and not his own. It was answered almost immediately. "Hershey, hi!" The words gushed out like a torrent. "I've done it. I've kicked Josh out."

"It's over, Claire," he said, cutting straight to the very sharp point.

Claire paused, hearing the words but not believing them. "What?"

"We're through."

"You can't be serious! We're the real thing!"

"I am and we're not."

"What about the contract?"

"What contract?"

"The contract you fucking signed for P&R PR to rebrand the Bank."

"Oh, *that* contract! It never existed."

There was a horrible silence as the enormity of what Hershey was telling her sank in.

"I'm going to lose my job," she whispered. "Patricia will fire me for this."

"What a pity," Hershey said, clearly not meaning a word of it.

"I've just dumped Josh."

"Maybe he'll take you back."

"I don't want him back."

"Then you're on your own."

"You fucking bastard," she hissed.

"You got that right!" he said and cut the call as Claire emitted a piercing shriek. He grinned, then crossed the last name off his list.

Culpepper was less than thrilled when his phone rang. He considered ignoring it, the sound was interrupting the minor pleasure he was deriving from watching the lights of the sporadic traffic flowing along the street far below him. But he couldn't do it; he was a man that needed to know what was going on all around him, all the time, to be in control of everything, even a telephone call.

He picked up the receiver. "Yes," he said tersely.

"Ian, it's me."

'Me' being Sir David Cowan, the most senior (in all respects) of the Bank's Board members and one of the few people Culpepper held a degree of respect for. And a measure of fear. Before Culpepper could respond Sir David ploughed on. "It's come to my attention the Bank is suffering a financial anomaly."

"What the fuck are you talking about, David?"

"It's *Sir* David," Cowan said and went on to explain what the fuck he was talking about.

When he'd finished reaming Culpepper out he abruptly ended the call. The Chairman dropped his mobile onto the surface of his desk with a thud, a death knell for sure. He'd been given the terrible news that there was sure to be a police investigation into embezzlement, bribery and corruption at the Bank, his Bank. There would be an Extraordinary Board Meeting in two days' time, to which he was being summoned to explain himself. The conversation was matter-of-fact, so much so that Culpepper knew he was right in the shit. A tight knot formed in the pit of his stomach, an utterly alien feeling of...dread. He forced it down and the horror blossomed into rage.

Even though Cowan hadn't said it outright he knew who'd been responsible for this. How fucking *dare* he, Culpepper raged. How could Valentine go up against him, the man who'd *made* the bastard into what he was? Everything Valentine had was due to him and him alone.

Well, he wasn't down and out, not just yet. He made a series of calls of his own, all on a second mobile he pulled out of his briefcase, the number of which only the closest of his close allies had. Valentine was going to pay. And in spades.

Hershey was shattered when he finally left his office. Shattered but at the same time utterly elated. With a few conversations he'd cut out every cancer in his corporate body and as a result given himself an unimpeded route to the very upper echelons of the Bank.

His phone rang. He sighed. Elodie again. He'd have to think of something to put her off, and permanently. Google would probably throw up something useful.

He grinned. He struggled to remember another day that had been so satisfying and so rewarding. *It was only up from here*, he thought as he rode the elevator down to the basement garage.

That's Not My Name

"This is it," I tell the cabbie.

I pay him then exit, slamming the door behind me. He drives his piece of French crap away in a puff of grey exhaust fumes. I'm on the edge of the estate, but I need the air. I walk down the road. I can hear the boom of the waves at the bottom of the cliffs. Periodically the beam of the lighthouse flickers over me, my shadow shrinks and elongates. Every lighthouse has a different pattern of lights. Apparently a sailor can tell where they are on the coast just by the pattern, like an SOS in morse.

Yes, my mind is wandering.

I stop outside the house. It looks like I'm in the right place but I've only been here once and that was in the daytime. However there aren't many residences on this very exclusive estate (they need the room around them for the expansive gardens and Olympic-sized swimming pools), so even if I'm not entirely on the money it won't take long to track Jack down, I tell myself. As I walk up the drive a light clicks on over the door. With a surprising fear of rejection I pause before knocking. This oddball guy I'd met on the train only a matter of weeks ago is my only hope. If he turns me away, I don't know what I'm going to do.

I raise a fist. Knuckles meet glossy paint twice. And a man I don't recognise opens the door. About my age, dark-haired, relatively unremarkable except for a very haughty look that cuts across his face.

"Yes?" the unknown man asks me, looking me up and down suspiciously as if I'm selling dusters door to door.

"Erm, I'm trying to find Jack?"

He shakes his head. "No Jack here," he says.

"That can't be right, I'm sure he lives here. In fact I was definitely here recently."

"You're mistaken." He starts to shut the door on me.

I put my hand out to stop him, my heart in my mouth. Something's amiss. "No, a young guy. Well-dressed, dark hair like you." It strikes me then that there's a resemblance between Jack and the man in front of me. "In fact a lot like you."

He laughs a short bark. "Then you probably mean my brother. But he's called Clive, not Jack."

"I don't know what you're talking about."

"Unfortunately I do. You'd better come in." He flings the door open wide.

I walk past him and into the same living room I'd sat in drinking with Jack, or whoever he is.

"Take a seat. My name's James by the way."

James, not Jim or Jimmy. One of those precise types then. I perch on the sofa and he sinks into the leather armchair opposite. I must admit I'm bloody puzzled and say so.

"Clive is a fantasist," James says by way of explanation. "He pretends he's someone else. Me, actually. He borrows my car, house, phone, suits, everything. Clive's never achieved anything in his life, he's a total failure. He's no friends, only me, no job, nothing."

"So, he doesn't work in London? Doesn't run his own business?"

James shakes his head. "As I said, nothing. He's a nobody."

I'm astonished. I'd guessed Jack/Clive/Whoever exaggerated to make himself look bigger and better than he actually was, but not that he's been pretending to be a completely different person.

"Does he owe you money?" James is asking. "That's why most people try to track him down."

"Money? No, I just need his help."

James burst out laughing, then says, "You must be fucked then."

I don't smile because he's one hundred and ten per cent correct. "Tell me where I can find him."

Another cab, another driver who looks warily about him. Late at night this part of Cliftonville isn't the nicest place to be. It's a downright shithole, to be honest. I don't want to be here either, I just don't have any choice.

I look again at the piece of paper and James's neat handwriting. "Drop me here please," I request. The driver doesn't need telling twice.

I hand over another note that I can ill afford (now I'm in the land of the unemployed) and get out of the car. The road stinks of shit, like so much of this area. Mingling with it is the aroma of a takeaway from some far-flung country. The immigrant population here is high. I'm in a minority and know it.

Up four crumbling steps to the front door. Once this would have been a grand house, like the area itself, which in the recent past had been home to hundreds of bustling hotels and B&B's, a major tourist venue. But it's all gone now and mutated into DSS accommodation for incomers that sponge off us taxpayers (I realise there's one blessing of losing my job — the tax man can fuck off).

There's a powerful waft of rotting waste. The front yard either side of the steps is a mess of overflowing bins. The seagulls have been into the rubbish bags and torn them apart, spewing out half-eaten food, nappies and all sorts of other shit I don't want to think about and that even the rats would think twice about before gnawing on. The recent heat hasn't helped, fusing everything together into a concoction Jamie Oliver wouldn't own up to. All in all, fucking disgusting.

Breathing through my mouth I look at the doorbells. There are eight of them. I try to read what's written on the little tags underneath each one. No Clive Hollowman there. Bollocks. Then I look again, something snagging my attention. In a font that a drunken spider dipped in ink would be pissed off with is the legend 'Jack Dean'. Jack is clearly living the pretence to the full. Fair enough. I lean on his bell for a full ten seconds. I can't hear it ring.

But what I do hear is some heavy, strangled breathing from behind me. It sounds like a rapist who's on the prowl, on the job or both. I reluctantly turn to see not the sexual deviant I expected, but a heavily-tattooed guy walking towards me with something that resembles a dog. The dog, if that's what it is, is straining on a leash and consequentially throttling itself. But it's had some really bad luck with the gene pool. Either that or it's been run over by a heavy truck several times. Whichever way it's a fucked-up beast shaped like a barrel, waddling with difficulty on four squat legs.

The guy stares at me as he nears. Then the dog suddenly lurches to a stop and crouches down for a shit right at the bottom of the steps. The guy still stares at me; I don't think he's blinked yet. I stupidly stare back. I know I shouldn't but there's something fascinating about him, in the way a circus freak show's fascinating.

He's as round as his dog, dressed in knee-length surf shorts and a cut-off T-shirt. I can imagine him wearing the same gear all year round, the misplaced macho type. My eyes are drawn to a tattoo, a snake that, well, snakes upwards from his ankles. The head that emerges from under his t-shirt at his neck has snarling fangs dripping blood. The man smiles at me, enjoying what must be my horror-laden look.

"It's continuous," he says to me, in a voice that's as heavy as he is. He licks his lips. "You can see if you like."

Fucking hell I'm being propositioned! I think.

"No, you're all right," I say, trying to pitch my tone at friendly and firm, but squeaky, weak and available emerges instead. I lean on the bell again. *For fuck's sake, come on Jack!*

"Don't you like snakes?" he says.

I shake my head. "Nope, scared to death of them, slimy bastards."

I turned back to the door and pressed the bell several times. Then press it again. I glance over my shoulder. Tattooed guy is still there, staring at me, making no effort to clear up the huge turd his beast has finished squeezing out.

"Well mine's not slimy at all," he replies, grabbing at his crotch and leaving me in no doubt as to what he was referring to, "and I only live round the corner so we could be back in five minutes. Your mate'd never even know you'd gone."

I swear my jaw drops open and smacks onto the top step with a whack. I'm rarely lost for words but I've truly no idea how to respond to this guy. Then, for the first time, and not the last, Jack appears to save me. The door cracks open and I squeeze through, like Indiana Jones escaping a tribe of natives baying for my blood.

"Josh!" he says, stunned at my appearance, apparently the last man he expects to see.

I push the door shut, relieved that Mr Tattoo will have to do his turd-burgling with someone else.

"Are you a sight for sore fucking eyes," I say, meaning every single word.

"So she threw you out?" Jack asks me, incredulous. I nod. "What a *bitch*."

We're sitting in his dingy bedsit. To say it's small would be the understatement of the century. You'd have to be a midget to live comfortably here, or an ant. The bedsit is located in the roof space, up four flights of stairs, so no wonder I couldn't hear the doorbell ring. The ceiling is canted at an impossible angle. It's baking hot, proving the insulation is poor, if not non-existent, and I bet it would be fucking freezing come the winter. There's a small kitchen space, with larder fridge and unit-top electric cooker, divided from the 'living' area by a breakfast bar so narrow a cup of tea would experience vertigo. The living area comprises two squashy, knackered chairs which we're currently occupying, a TV my grandfather would have been proud of and a single bed. Storage space is built into the sloping walls, if the handles periodically spaced are anything to go by. There's also a small bathroom, Jack tells me, although at this time I haven't been inside to check out the facilities. I can't imagine it being any more capacious though. Submariners in the Second World War probably lived better than this. Jack looks at me, unsure what to say or do next. He's clearly very uncomfortable, relatively poorly dressed in grey tracksuit bottoms and a mangy T-shirt.

"I expect you're wondering why I'm staying here?" Jack asks.

"No."

"It's a friend's flat that I'm looking after," Jack says, ignoring my monosyllabic assertion.

"I spoke to your brother," I say. It's as if I've pronounced a death sentence. The high colour in his face immediately drains away, like a light snapping out.

"Oh."

"He told me everything. The pretence, the pseudonym, everything."

"Oh. Shit."

He stands up and then sits down again; he's nowhere to retreat to. He stands and goes to the fridge, jerks it open and pulls out a beer. He snaps the ring pull and downs the can in one draft. Dropping the empty in the bin he opens the fridge and takes another.

"Everything?" he asks, wiping his chin.

I nod. Jack bolts down the second beer. The fridge door opens to another beer. At this rate he'll be shitfaced within the next five minutes.

"Look, I can explain," he starts.

I interrupt, raising a hand to stop the flow before it can begin.

"I don't give a flying fuck," I say, "I just want somewhere to crash. I've no one else and I need your help. Your reasons are your own."

Jack stares at me, unbelieving, a rabbit in the headlights waiting for a bullet in the brain.

"Calling you Clive seems a bit weird. Do you mind if I call you Jack?"

He puts the unopened beer can on the work surface. "The chair's going spare," he says.

"Don't think this means we're friends again."

Jack looks gutted but I don't care.

Over the next hour I give Jack the whole nine yards — my suspension for alleged (bullshit) embezzlement, my drunken route home to find out I've been evicted and finally the text from Claire dumping me. I'm fucking miserable. My entire world has come crashing down around me.

Jack, already pale, goes as white as a ghost again as my story unfolds. He looks genuinely shocked. I must admit I'm touched by his empathy. It's not until much, much later that I understand the true source of his awkwardness.

When I've finished my sorry tale he sits open-mouthed for a whole minute. Then with real feeling he says, "I'll sort it out for you, mate. Really I will."

"Thanks, I appreciate it, but frankly I'm not sure what you can do for me. I'm in the shit. All I really need right now is a place to crash."

"Leave it to me. You look knackered. Why don't you get some sleep? Take my bed."

I realise I'm shattered. I don't argue and throw myself on Jack's tiny bed. I'm sure I'm asleep instantly.

Wind Back The Clock

Jack's fingers flew over the keyboard, the rattle of the keys sounding like a hundred tap dancers. He'd sat still as a tree for a full five minutes after Josh had gone to bed, letting the enormity of what he'd done to his friend sink into his bones. The promise he'd made to himself to look after Josh no matter what had been shattered. And all because of his ego, the feeling that at last his unique talents were being appreciated and he was being rewarded well for them. But he'd been blinded by his desire to please his paymaster, and all the time he was attacking his one and only friend.

First Jack had gone to his management books, flicked to the index and looked up his problem, dropping them one by one onto the floor as he found each book of no value. None listed 'betrayal' or 'friend' in the index. The books had gone into a bin bag. He got pissed off and pulled open a cupboard, extracted his suit. It had followed the books, so had ties, shirt, pen, watch, everything associated with his 'business'. He carried the bag down four flights of stairs, yanked open the front door and dropped it on top of the rest of the stinking rubbish.

Once back upstairs and behind closed doors he'd booted up his computer, entered the account details from memory (which was photographic) and transferred all of the money back out. Then he'd covered up his tracks, backed out of the programme secure that no one would ever know he'd been there or that Josh's account had been tainted. Any activity would be looked on as an aberration, a ghost in the machine, a gremlin.

As the flare of the computer screen died he pushed his seat back and rubbed his eyes, feeling more drained than he ever had in his life. He just hoped he'd done enough and done it soon enough.

Time would tell.

Nicked

The police come for me the next day. It isn't like in the cop shows on TV, not at all. There's a hard knock, four beats from a heavy hand. Jack isn't in to answer it (more beer needed) so I ignore whoever it is. But they're insistent bastards because the hammering continues, so I reluctantly shuffle over to the door, open it just a crack in case there's a weirdo the other side. No, just two scruffy men in badly-fitting suits. One has his ID raised.

"Guy Gregory, CID," he says, "And this is Kevin Piper." Piper also raises his ID for me to inspect. "We'd like to ask you some questions down the station."

"Do I have a choice?" I ask.

Gregory smiles. "Not really, no."

Ten minutes later I'm dressed and in the back of an unmarked car. It's only a short drive along the High Street, a right past Aldi then left onto the esplanade that runs parallel to the sea. I look briefly at the Winter Gardens as we pass by, an Edwardian theatre sunk into the cliffs which had its best days at least forty years ago, before a sharp left turn into the cop shop. I'm signed in by Piper whilst Gregory disappears within. Then I'm in a small, plain interview room at a desk with a man I don't recognise.

He introduces himself to the recording device. "DCI Meadows. Interview with Mr Josh Dedman. Time is...11.11am." Meadows smiles, as if the time is something special.

"Have I been arrested?" I ask.

Meadows smiles again, he seems to like doing that. Or he's had a training course on relationship-building for coppers. "No, we're just hoping you'll help us with our enquiries."

"Do I need a lawyer?"

He shrugs. "No, unless you're guilty of course."

"I haven't done anything."

"We'll decide that. A rather large sum of money has gone missing and your employer is trying to understand where it's gone and who's taken it."

"I've no idea what you're talking about."

"Your employer thinks you do." Meadows opens a file and slides a piece of paper over to me. "Do you recognise this?"

I pick up the paper and glance at it briefly. "Sure. It's my bank statement."

He takes another piece of paper out of his folder and places it on the table in front of me beside its friend. "And this?"

"Same," I say, barely registering what appears to be an identical document.

"Why don't you look a little closer. Specifically here." He taps the paper, drawing my attention to the credit.

£20,000,000.00.

"Fucking hell," I breathe, absolutely not believing what I'm seeing. I drag my focus away from the eye-watering sum and to Meadows's face. "I'll get that lawyer now please."

"I thought you'd say that."

And then he nicks me.

I'm taken back to my cell whilst I await a lawyer, to be provided gratis by the state. A lunch of tasteless pulp is delivered, but I barely touch it. For the rest of the afternoon I'm periodically interviewed by Meadows, with breaks for refreshment or a discussion with my lawyer, whose name I can't remember. It's relatively pointless stuff; I know nothing about the money so I've nothing I can tell them. But Meadows believes the statement to be irrefutable evidence of my guilt and the expression on his face tells me so every time I deny knowledge of its existence.

Eventually I get pissed off and clam up. I refuse to answer any more questions. Meadows gets his own back by banging me up in the cell. My lawyer seems incapable or unwilling to get me out, which secretly I'm quite pleased with because it's in effect a night out. So I'm stuck here, thankfully all alone because the last thing I need is tattoo man or, worse, his dog to show up...

Damage Limitation

The phone on Culpepper's desk rattled. "I thought I'd fucking told you, no more calls!" he shouted, before remembering he'd sent his secretary home for the night. The fewer people who knew what was going on, the better.

He sighed and picked it up. "What."

"Mr Culpepper? This is David Brodie from The Times."

"I don't speak to reporters."

"I'm very familiar with your habits, sir, but I was wondering whether you'd care to comment on the story we're about to run of a scandal brewing within your Bank."

Culpepper froze and gripped the receiver tightly, mouth open in astonishment.

"Mr Culpepper? Did you know one of your employees, a Mr Dedman, has been detained by the police? Do you have a comment to make at all?" Brodie's thin voice asked again.

"I've no idea what you're talking about." Culpepper said, and put the phone down very gently.

He grabbed his private mobile, pressed a single button to get hold of Mr Lamb. He needed to know *exactly* what was going on, because his statement had been true. He really didn't have a clue what Broadie was talking about. He barked his demands and gave Mr Lamb five minutes to call back, which he did. Exactly on time.

"Tell me what the fuck is happening," Culpepper demanded.

"It's true. Our boy has been arrested," Mr Lamb said.

"When?"

"This morning."

"*This morning?* Why am I only finding out now?" Culpepper spat. There was silence on the line in response. "Any charges?"

"Yes, obstructing the course of justice. It's an attempt to hold him a bit longer."

"Right, I'll sort this out. Seems to me I'm the only fucking one that gets things done round here. In the meantime get your arse down there. I need you on the ground."

Mr Lamb didn't reply because he'd already cut the connection, which Culpepper took as an acknowledgement.

"Can you speak?" Culpepper asked when the call was answered. There was the sound of a party in the background, raised voices and laughter.

"Give me a moment," the man said. The revelry noises evaporated, replaced by a gusting wind.

"I need your help with a little problem," Culpepper said, then explained the situation. Finally he said, "Get him released. Immediately."

"That won't be easy."

"What the fuck do I care? Just get it done." Culpepper disconnected the call and put the phone back in his pocket. "Fucking idiot."

Eighty miles away and two minutes later DCI Meadows's mobile rang. He ignored it. He'd had a shitty long day and couldn't be bothered with anything other than getting some sleep. The ringtone died for all of five seconds before it started up again. Meadows let the phone ring itself out, then turned it off.

"I can't get through to the right person."

"That's fucking ridiculous!" Culpepper exploded.

"It'll have to wait until morning."

"But it can't, it has to be dealt with now! Get hold of someone else."

"Ian, if you want this contained the last thing to do is start contacting all and sundry. I'll get hold of Meadows first thing and chew his balls off. It'll be sorted tomorrow, I promise."

"It had fucking better be or it's your balls I'll be after." Culpepper slammed the phone down.

He flopped back in his chair. It was going to be a long night; there was no way he was going to hitting the sack any time soon because if the Met's Commissioner couldn't help then no one could.

DCI Meadows got to Margate nick at 8.30am. He hadn't slept well. The seagulls around here were the size of Labradors and ten times noisier. He'd got himself a coffee (instant) before he remembered to switch his mobile back on. Within moments it rang. He answered, took the angry blast straight in the ear, listened to the brief order, frowned, confirmed that he understood the command and disconnected the call.

He sighed in frustration. First he'd had to deal with the visitor who'd stared at him blankly through the glass divide in the reception area. Meadows had been around long enough to recognise the type, the bible-black eyes always gave them away, but this guy had been on a whole new level. And then the call he'd just taken. From bad to worse to utter shite.

"Ah fuck it," he said and went to get Dedman from the cells.

That's What Enemies Are For

They kick me out first thing in the morning, as near as dammit telling me to sod off.

"What's going on?" I ask Meadows, who looks less than pleased.

"We're letting you go."

"I don't understand."

"You've friends in high places. You're a lucky lad."

I still don't understand. I really haven't any friends, even in low places.

"Whereas I, on the other hand," continues Meadows, "am very unlucky. I've had to spend a day in this dump you call home and now I have to go back to London with nothing to show for my efforts. What a fucking waste of time."

"Is that it?"

"Unfortunately yes." He leans in close to me, his breath on my face, pungent with stale coffee. "But I hate getting hauled off a case, so pray we don't meet again."

And with that I'm bundled out of the interview room, through the station and onto the street. I stand there in the car park letting the wind off the sea slap me in the face, in an attempt to counteract the somewhat dazed feeling.

"Josh, over here!" calls a familiar voice. I look around, searching for the source.

"What are you doing here?"

"I heard you'd been arrested and came down as soon as I could. Sorry I'm a bit late, train was delayed," Liam says.

If you'd have asked me to write a list of ten people I expected to see there and then, Liam wouldn't be on it.

"That's pretty normal, but it doesn't matter, they've just let me go without charge so you've had a bit of a wasted journey."

"Really?" He pauses a moment and says, "I think that's you."

It takes me a few moments to realise my leg is ringing and vibrating in succession. I pull my phone out and answer.

"I hear you've been let off." An American drawl, irritatingly confident.

"Hershey," I mouth at Liam and he raises an eyebrow.

"Yes."

"You lucky bastard!"

"That's the second time I've been called that in as many minutes."

"Yeah? Is that so?" Hershey says in my ear. "Anyhoo, I didn't call to be pleasant."

"Great, thanks."

"Hey, don't mention it."

"So, what the fuck do you want?" I'm getting angry now. Everything that's happening to me feels displaced, wrong, like it should be someone else's problem and not mine.

"Hey, no need to be rude. For the moment I'm still your boss, you know." Hershey tries to sound hurt, but fails. The guy doesn't possess a single emotion that isn't self-motivated.

"Hershey, tell me what you want or *fuck off*."

"Well, okay, but remember it was you that asked me."

"I'm going, Valentine. Goodbye."

"It was just to let you know I've been screwing your girlfriend."

There's a heavy pause and heavier breathing from my end of the line. There's just me, a phone and Hershey in the whole world right now. "You've been doing what?" I ask quietly.

"*Screwing Claire!* Hey, apologies for shouting, it was just in case you didn't hear me the first time around."

Oh, I hear him all right. A lot of things start to click into place, except one, so I ask. "Why?"

"Simple really. I fucking hate you, man. Always have, always will. I just thought you'd like to know. Oh and by the way, I'll be running the Bank soon and even if the cops have let you off, I haven't ,so don't think you'll be coming back to your job at any time in the future."

Before I get the chance to tell Hershey what an arsehole I think he is and what I'm going to do to him he ends the call.

I Spy

On the opposite side of the road from the police station Konstantin slouched on a bench, a vodka bottle by his side. He smelled and looked drunk but was utterly sober. He didn't like what and who he was seeing. He raised his phone and zoomed in.

Click.

Revenge Is A Dish Best Served Drunk

It's incredible how much the average man can sulk. Such a small word, *sulk*, only four letters, but with such a dam of emotion stooping behind it. Here I sit in Jack's dingy little bedsit. I don't think of him as Clive, to me he remains Jack, which he's delighted with. Apparently I'm the first person that his nom de plume has stuck with.

I'm not sure the last time I washed or ate or got dressed. Days? Fuck knows. Could be weeks for all I care. My boxers feel like they are glued to my body. All I wear is Claire's old T-shirt and the pink, frilly, short-sleeved dressing gown I bought her for Christmas. I'd found them in the rubbish bags that Jack had collected from outside my ex-flat.

I am bloody tired although I've done nothing but sleep, mostly in Jack's reclining chair. Jack himself has rarely left the bedsit, spending most of his time with me. The London trips look like they've been knocked on the head. I say he's been 'with' me but I've largely ignored anything he's said. He doesn't seem to care. He treats me like a coma patient, constantly making conversation and observations (i.e. bullshit). He picks up all my crap, recycles all the beer cans and vodka bottles, flushes the toilet behind me, brings me cups of tea (I hate tea so they go cold) and sandwiches (which I ignore and they dry up). If I was on my own the liquid and solid refreshments would soon be growing interesting collections of fungi on them.

"The trouble is," Jack's saying, "You've no frame of reference anymore."

What the *fuck* is he on about now? The incomprehension must show on my face because Jack smiles. The patient has shown a flicker of emotion. Success!

"No job, no girlfriend," Jack says.

"Bitch," I interrupt.

Keep going Dr Dean! The nurses swoon with the euphoria of success after continual failure to get through to the patient!

"No house, no money and no friends, besides me and a Russian tramp." Jack blinks in realisation. "Wow, that's pretty shit really."

I want to scream, "*Thanks, that really helped!*" But I stay mute and stare unblinking at daytime TV. If anything can euthanise the brain, this is it. Jack and meaningless, shit TV.

"I read a book once. It said that revenge was a great way of dealing with your troubles," Jack says, then crosses his eyebrows in thought.

Revenge, the word tickles my synapses. A slightly larger word than sulk, but with many more layers of associated passion.

"Or did it say revenge was *bad*?" Jack says, completely throwing himself off balance.

But it's too late. Waaaaay too late for *that* genie to be stuffed back in the bottle.

"You're a fucking genius, Jack," I say. He grins at me. Dr Dean has saved the day, again!

I fairly leap out of my chair. Bits of me ache, my muscles have atrophied somewhat after the (unknown) fallow period. I catch a whiff of something unsavoury and sniff my armpit.

"God, I fucking stink. I need a shower." Then I realise I'm wearing Claire's shit. "And these pieces of crap can go in the bin."

I strip off, dumping the pink dressing gown and flowery T-shirt on the floor. The chastity boxers follow. I stand in the middle of Jack's tiny bedsit stark bollock naked. He doesn't know where to look.

But I don't care.

I feel great.

I'm going to kill that bastard Valentine...

Many Reasons To Die

Claire went through the seven stages of grief in seven days. She'd won and lost a lucrative contract she'd never had and with it her job, dumped a long-term boyfriend (okay, maybe that wasn't so bad) and been dumped herself by her short-term fuck buddy (which was). On the seventh day she saw that she and Hershey really were over, that she and Hershey had never been and had never been meant to be. What finally brought her to a constructive conclusion was the icy decision that Hershey himself should never be. All she needed to decide was when and how to kill the bastard...

Elodie, being French, was incapable of icy calm. Instead she was a whirlpool of emotions, like a hyperactive teenager on a bunch of Class As. She had no idea how she was going to feel from one moment to the next — fury, jealousy, anguish, all at the same time and one after the other. But chasing them through was a series of other emotions, like panic, fear and loathing. After many attempts she'd finally managed to speak to Hershey. She'd got confused and had to Google the phrase he'd used — switch-hitter. It didn't mean anything to her in French or English. Once the search engine had found a suitable translation she'd gone cold to her marrow and understood why Hershey had advised her to get a test as soon as possible — a switch-hitter was someone who fucked men as well as women. Elodie knew there was only one way to make herself feel better and that was to kill Hershey. She still had a key to his house so getting in would be easy. Va te faire foutre, enculé...

Culpepper, being a banker, was as bereft of emotion as a corpse is of life. He was absolutely clear what he had to do, which was to ensure Valentine got dead, and fucking fast. The decisions that followed were how much to pay and who to choose. It couldn't be Mr Lamb, he wasn't the killing kind these days. He knew a few bent coppers; maybe they would do it...

Konstantin was excited. It had been some time since he'd murdered a man. He liked being up close and personal. Guns made too much noise. He preferred a knife or, best of all, his hands. Getting into Hershey's house would be no obstacle. He grinned and flexed his fingers, like a power lifter preparing for a gold medal lunge. The whole thing was going to be fun and, best of all, he was helping a friend, who'd never be any the wiser if all went to plan...

Jack was utterly petrified. He didn't want to kill Hershey but he knew he had to, for his one and only friend. He was certain that if Josh did the deed then he would lose him and he couldn't face the idea of being alone again. He looked at his hands. They shook like a force nine earthquake rattled buildings, merciless and unstoppable. He had no idea how he was going to kill Hershey, he just knew it had to be soon. He dashed to the bathroom and threw up.

A Taste of Death in My Mouth

One thing I've finally learnt at the tender age of twenty-nine is to love every minute that you have. Enjoy everything, even if it's shit, because a shit moment is a hell of a lot better than being dead. Ask Hershey. He'll tell you that. If he could. But more of that in a moment.

I'm standing — more accurately, swaying — outside Hershey's house. I'm not an architect, but I can appreciate fine buildings and this is certainly grand. It's tall, narrow and elegant with stone steps up to the front door. It has a basement flat below street level (I can see the tops of the windows) and three more floors above it with sash windows to allow plenty of light in. Very nice, just the sort of place I'd like to live in myself one day.

I'd thrown down a lot of alcohol on the train into London, keeping myself topped up. Dutch courage, you ask? No, not at all. I've grown to like the feeling of being numb, of everything being slow, to like it that thoughts have to push through a rubbery gauze to make it into my mind. However the downside is when I'm thinking about the best way to gain access to Hershey's place, because my pickled brain fucks it up. Ultimately, now I'm faced with Hershey's front door, I can only settle upon the direct route, so I simply stagger up the steps and ring the bell. I figure that everyone answers the door, so when he lets me in we'll talk and eventually I'll kill him, although at this stage I haven't considered the difficult question: How? I don't know. I'm just utterly certain that I will murder the bastard, and the drink is convincing me I'll be successful.

But there's already one fatal flaw in my grand plan. Hershey doesn't answer. I stand impotently on the top step waiting. I ring the bell again, knock. Nothing. But I'm sure I hear movement inside. I press my ear to the door and then knock again. An old woman walking a rat on a leash looks at me quizzically as she idles past. I ignore her, but I know I can't stand here forever, and I'm not leaving. Consequently I'm in a difficult position. So I try the door handle. Against all expectations it's unlocked and swings open easily. I glance over my shoulder as I enter; the woman is looking at me through narrowed eyes. I close the door on her and her stupid fucking dog.

I find myself in a gloomy hall. The sound of the outside world is gone. Excellent insulation. Once my eyes adjust I can see indistinct shadows of furniture. The house is deceptively large. There are several closed doors, a set of stairs down and a set of stairs up. A red light blinks to my right on a cabinet beside the front door. I pick up Hershey's horribly flashy phone. If this is here, he certainly is. As I replace the Blackberry I think I hear a noise above me. I cock my head and listen, but there's nothing. Perhaps I imagined it.

I decide to descend first. I like the idea of basements, seeing people's feet as they walk by, oblivious to me looking up. Two worlds close by but disconnected. The steep steps lead down to a wooden door, which is closed. I feel the temperature drop slightly. I listen at the door. Nothing. I fumble for the catch, lift it and push the door open, heart in my mouth. The door swings into a decent space — whitewashed walls, a sofa, hi-fi and a large fireplace. The curtains are wide open and there's sudden brightness in the stairwell. It's obviously an area for relaxing, but there's no one taking it easy. I go back up the stairs, leaving the door open for a bit of light. Once back in the corridor I walk along it as stealthily as I can (which isn't saying much) trying each door in turn. None give when I twist the handle and push. All locked up then. Hershey must have a perversely introverted sense of security, but maybe that's because he's American.

The same is true on the first floor and on most of the second until I reach what is clearly the formal living area. It's very different to the basement, like the house had two interior designers on a reality TV show — one casual and understated, the other utterly over the top and a pure reflection of status and money. This room, dimly lit because the curtains are drawn, reflects the latter. There's a huge plasma screen and home cinema system, leather sofa, Bose hi-fi, expensive pieces of furniture, rich mahogany flooring with a thick, probably Persian rug on top, a chandelier.

And a body.

Whodunnit?

Claire felt giddy. The sight of all the blood and gore had been much worse than she'd expected. She'd also been surprised that Hershey actually had brains, but the evidence of their presence was there for all to see, which was when she'd vomited...

Elodie hadn't really understood what had happened at first, but Hershey was dead. She didn't know much about anything (she was French, after all) but she knew she was in trouble. Big trouble...

Konstantin was somewhat disappointed. What a basic way to kill someone. There was no finesse. Murder should be something akin to art, otherwise Konstantin felt he was no better than a simple butcher, slaughtering a dumb animal. But on the other hand he recognised that speed was of the essence and that was sometimes all that mattered. So he shrugged and put up with it...

Jack was delighted Hershey was dead. He felt a huge sense of relief, a weight the size of London lifted from his shoulders. He could stand tall again. It was over, everything would be straightforward now. Let's be honest, nothing in the rest of his life could be as problematic as getting up the nerve to kill someone...

Mr Lamb hadn't yet done what he'd come here to do. He had to wait until he was alone. Until then he simmered. No, he was *furious*. He'd never had such a strong emotion in his life; it was odd to have a feeling. Mr Lamb knew this was all getting too far out of control. It had to stop, but right now he couldn't figure out how to bring everything to a satisfactory conclusion. He stood back from the window, watching the street but out of sight as he thought...

Yes, They Are Grey

The room reeks of vomit, blood and shit. I swear there's still the faint odour of the gunshot that had taken away part of Hershey's skull. I lie on the floor and cover my face with my arm, but it does little to keep the stench out of my nostrils. As it permeates my body the alcohol is forced out of my bloodstream at the same pace. I sober up bloody quickly, I can tell you.

I fully appreciate that if the cops catch me here I'll be in serious trouble, not quite as much as Hershey, but enough. Only a matter of days ago I'd been in custody and accused of defrauding my employer. It's well known at the Bank that I hate Hershey. The police aren't stupid and I'm sure they'd put two and two together pretty quickly and come knocking on my door again. So I have to do something, I can't just lie here and decompose steadily along with the bastard.

I pick myself up off the floor and pull out my mobile. The charge is low but the screen lights up the room, throwing the corpse into relief. I almost press the speed dial key for Claire but hold back. Instead I take the back off then pull the battery out. I've seen enough television to know the police can triangulate a location. I'm desperate to make a call, but I know I'll have to save it for later.

My mind is screaming at me to get out of the house *now*, but a morbid curiosity overcomes my good sense. Hershey has been the cause of so much shit in my life I have to make sure he really is dead, even though it's fucking obvious. I cross slowly to the wing back chair he reclines in, breathing through my mouth to keep the worst of the stiff's perfume at bay. His bowels must have relaxed with his expiration; the leather is stained with shit and piss. He's slouched slightly, his head tipped to one side, his jaw slack. There's a small hole in one temple and a much larger exit wound at the back of his head, blood and brains all over the chair and wall behind. The bullet looks to have gone in at an angle.

One of his arms lies across his lap; the other has flopped down and hangs over the side of the chair. Something is bothering me so I kneel down and look underneath the wing back, which stands well above the floor on four ornate wooden legs. There's a drying pool of piss, but no gun.

Then I freeze. I hear movement downstairs, I'm sure the front door opens. I run out of the living room, leaving Hershey alone, to the window at the end of the corridor. I press my face against the cool glass and look in both directions, but I can't see anyone. Then my nerve breaks. I have to get out of here. I run down the stairs. The front door yawns open. Someone else was definitely in the house.

Backfill

Mr Lamb watched them exit one by one. Amazingly all seemed utterly unaware of the others. He knew all of them, including the badly dressed man, even though he kept his face hidden and affected a limp. Last to depart was Josh. He went up and down the steps several times then wandered uncertainly along the pavement. It took him a full minute to travel about a hundred yards, some internal turmoil apparently gripping him. Mr Lamb could well understand why. He wanted to be well away himself but waited in the shadow of the window a full five minutes once Josh finally was out of sight. Then he completed his task and headed out via the back door and along a narrow alley. Over his shoulder was slung a bag containing Hershey's Blackberry and laptop. Both would be searched, cleaned and put into his office at the Bank, and no one would be any the wiser, particularly the police. But first Mr Lamb wanted to take a look at any data on the hard drive himself.

After a measured fifteen minute walk the apartment was a mile away and Mr Lamb was in a far seedier part of town with a much larger criminal element where he could happily blend into the background. It was where he had spent his youth, after all.

He tapped the number he had memorised into the keypad, calling one throwaway mobile phone from another. The dial tone rang once in his ear before it was answered, as if the person on the other end was waiting only for this call, which Mr Lamb knew was entirely the case.

"The business is concluded," he said.

"You're later than planned. Were there issues?"

No 'congratulations', no 'well done.' Mentally Mr Lamb shrugged, it was typical.

"No, everything was as expected," he lied, another unfamiliar action.

"Are you *certain*?"

He felt a moment's irritation; his word and reputation should be enough. "I have already confirmed that to be the case," he replied, steel in his tone.

There was a momentary silence before he was answered. "Good. Then I will ensure the details are concluded at my end."

The connection was broken. He deleted the call memory and powered down the phone before crushing the cheap plastic underfoot. The sharp crack as it shattered went unnoticed. He scooped the shards of casing and electronic board up, deposited them in a nearby bin and walked away.

Culpepper tapped the mobile phone on his chin, pleased that at last he could end this sorry business. Of course there would be a lavish funeral for one of his top employees. Already he was framing the eulogy in his mind — 'our best and brightest cruelly taken from us in his prime', or some such bollocks. Another couple of calls to movers and shakers in high places to close the loop and he could head back to his home and a well-deserved crystal tumbler of something malt and at least 40 degrees proof. The phone reception here was crap, out in the sticks and well away from anyone.

He frowned as a ringtone broke his deserved contemplation. It wasn't the throwaway in his hand, but his own personal phone tucked in his pocket. Damn, he'd forgotten to turn it off. He pulled out the phone and swore as he recognised the number.

"I thought I told you not to call me unless it's critical," Culpepper barked.

"It is critical," came back the retort from Edward Shoe, the Bank's FD. "The money's not where Hershey said it was."

Culpepper could swear he felt his balls shrink with the news. "Are you certain?"

"I wouldn't be telling you if I wasn't," Shoe replied indignantly. Culpepper noted it was the second time in three minutes he'd been reprimanded by employees. That would be dealt with, but later.

"Do you know where it is?"

"Not yet, I've got someone working on it. All I know is, it's not where it's supposed to be any more."

"Holy fuck," Culpepper breathed. The game wasn't quite over then.

"Hopefully there will be some useful data on the laptop we can mine," Shoe said, not sounding convincing.

"Keep working on it. Let me know the instant you find something."

"On this number?" Shoe asked.

"Yes you prick!" Culpepper disconnected the call, a degree of balance in their relationship restored. He sat breathing heavily, heart thumping, vainly trying to calm himself. The money was missing and the Bank still perilously close to the edge of collapse but Valentine couldn't be asked where the money had gone.

Culpepper sat stock still, his mind in submission. For once he didn't have a clue what to do next.

Mr Lamb remained unhappy as he clambered into his car. He didn't like what he was being asked to do, it was beneath him and dangerous. He felt compromised, put upon and horribly exposed. He decided this would be his last job for Culpepper, he could find someone else to do his grubby work. He was sure there wouldn't be a shortage of takers. The pay was good enough.

His conscience proved an irritation until he started the engine, hauled on the steering wheel and performed a rapid 180° turn. It only took a brief grid search to find him. Josh was conspicuous, unconscious and far too close to Hershey's house for comfort. Mr Lamb ensured no one was watching and bundled Dedman into his car, laying him flat on the rear seat. It never ceased to amaze Mr Lamb how utterly unaware the general public were. As he pulled away a police car, its lights flashing, whizzed past in the opposite direction. Mr Lamb suspected he knew where it was heading.

He drove Dedman until they were well away from the scene. He saw somewhere suitable, took a left and bumped along an alley. Twenty yards down and well into the shadows he drew up. Leaving the engine running he opened the rear door, lifted Josh out, carried him to the other side into a recessed doorway and set him carefully down. After a moment's reconsideration he took a blanket from his boot and put it around Josh's shoulders to keep him warm.

This isn't good, he thought, I'm becoming sentimental.

Then he was back in the car. A quick glance up and down the road to ensure the route was clear and he was gone.

Mr Lamb pulled into the car park of a large, anonymous supermarket. He booted up the laptop and started searching for anything of value. It didn't take long. He shut the computer down, closed the lid and slid it back into the rucksack. He started the engine and exited, decision made.

Shoe would be getting a visit later.

Sole Music

I'm bloody freezing and I ache from head to toe, as if I've been sleeping on something hard, which I soon discover that I have. It's pouring. The cold raindrops on my face are what's revived me. I raise my head an inch or so off the floor and look around blearily. I seem to be in an alley, lying on the floor with a damp blanket over me. A strong smell of urine and vomit assaults my nostrils. Parts of me I didn't even know I had are throbbing. I've the mother of all hangovers. I'm confused because I've absolutely no idea how I got here. There's a hazy memory of Hershey's body slumped in his chair, but beyond that? Nothing. Was it a dream? I shake my muggy head to clear out the cobwebs. With difficulty I stand up, the blanket dropping off me. Quite a well-made and expensive one too by the look of it, but then I'm no rug expert. I push myself further back into the doorway to get out of the rain coming down at a steep angle.

I feel like I should get out of here (even accepting the fact that alleys aren't my usual haunt) but a quick inspection of my pockets reveals no money and a phone. I'm amazed I haven't been robbed or sexually assaulted whilst unconscious. I need help. After a bit more patting I find the battery and rebuild my mobile. It takes a few minutes for the phone to boot up and find a network. I start to shiver, then the provider's logo appears briefly on screen, then my background photo and the signal bars drop in, the satellite's finger just about managing to touch me between the tall buildings. The photo's of Claire. I need to change that.

Who can I call? I have no one, not one real friend in the world. Recent events have proved that. But being a friend isn't a requirement for the job, anyone with transport will do. I snap my fingers as a light bulb blinks into existence over my head. Brilliant idea — Liam, I'll ring Liam. Not a friend as such but he's solid, dependable and that'll do for me. I scroll down, find his number and call. It goes straight to voicemail. Oh, for fuck's sake.

My head jackhammers again with the surge of adrenaline. When it calms to a mere pounding I scroll through the contacts on my phone, down then up. Twice. It doesn't take long. I sigh. That's it then, I'm down to Jack. Not solid, not dependable, not even someone I particularly like at this moment in time, but there's no one else. Really no one else. I ring, he answers and, to be fair, agrees to help without question. I should be pleased but instead I'm just more worried than ever because he's such a fuck up.

Fifteen bone-quaking minutes later and I'm climbing into Jack's car, or more accurately his brother's Range Rover. It's big, black and reeks of leather and air freshener. Jack jerks to the alley's end, then stalls as he attempts to pull out into the road. A pedestrian glares.

"Shit, I can't get used to this thing," he says, twisting the key in the ignition.

"I'm amazed your brother lent it to you," I say.

"He didn't. I needed a car fast and so I borrowed it."

The engine's running again and Jack nudges the beast into a gap.

"Nicked it you mean."

He shrugs. "Appropriated. Anyway, there's something you should know. Hershey's dead. Apparent suicide." He avoids my gaze. He looks tense, sweat a sheen on his forehead. "The police are all over the place and I've been looking everywhere for you."

"Why would you be looking for me?"

"We're friends and I owe you."

"We're not friends and yes, as a matter of fact you do."

"You called me, remember?"

I grunt and lean my head against the window, enjoying its coolness. "I'm not in the fucking mood."

Jack slams the brakes on, bringing the big car to a rapid halt. The tyres squeal as they bite through the wet to the tarmac. I bang my head. A peel of horns blasts out and Jack gives some guy the finger as he overtakes, eliciting a further honk. "Why are you being such an arsehole?" he demands, a look of pure anger on his face.

I'm shocked. This is a side to Jack I've not seen before, the first time he's properly lost his temper with me. I can see he means it.

"If the police had found you anywhere near Hershey's house you'd be an immediate suspect. I've been trying to help you for fuck's sake," he bellows.

Any remaining energy I have drains out of me there and then. Here am I berating someone for merely looking out for my worthless soul. "Look, I'm really sorry Jack. I've just woken up in an alley. I'm wet and cold. Last night I was ready to kill the bastard and instead I find somebody got there first. Frankly I'm pretty fucked up right now."

"Apology accepted," he says, his voice slightly calmer. He glances into his wing mirrors to check the road is clear. He flicks on an indicator.

"Can you take us by his place please?"

"Are you mad? Didn't you hear me say the cops are everywhere?" Jack's tone is up a pitch again.

"I just want to make sure it's all real."

"Oh it's fucking real all right, believe me."

"Please."

He shakes his head then stabs at the built-in satnav. Hershey's address is already programmed in, which strikes me as odd, but an ambulance and a cop car whip past, their lights splashing blue, distracting my attention. Thankfully the windows are tinted and a badly-parked car was apparently the least of their concerns right now. Once the instructions are on screen Jack pulls back out into the traffic (no indicating, another blare of horns) and within minutes we're at the end of the leafy avenue on which Hershey's house is located. It's blocked off by a couple of police cars parked in an arrowhead pointing outwards. There are reporters and television crews milling about, talking to camera, talking to each other, talking to neighbours. In the distance white-suited forensic officers move in and out of the house.

"Please tell me you've seen enough," Jack pleads.

A thoroughly soaked-through and pissed-off-looking constable starts to walk in our direction, obviously ready to move us on and probably in a fashion that will cheer him up a great deal and me not at all.

"Yeah, let's get the fuck out of here," I say, and Jack gratefully pulls away with a jerk.

It's a slow journey home. There seem to be police on every corner as we trek across London. Almost every time we stop Jack stalls, missing several traffic lights in the process and pissing every third driver off. London can be a very angry place at times. I withdraw into myself as he concentrates on the road and his clutch gremlin, so I'm able to spend a lot of time thinking. And the more I think, the more I worry. I consider every scenario imaginable and then a further few. The more I deliberate the darker and more dangerous the outcome develops into.

"We're here," Jack says. I look around; we are indeed outside his flat. The engine ticks as it cools. I must have nodded off.

"Can you go and open up the flat, Jack?"

"Eh?"

"Just open the fucking door will you. I don't want anyone to see me."

He shrugs and gets out of the Range Rover, his earlier anger seemingly burnt out. He drops the monumental height from the driver's seat, runs across the pavement, up the flat's steps, unlocks the door and pushes it open. Once the way is clear I jump out of the beast and sprint the short distance through the glaring sunlight and into the cool, dank hallway, as if I'm some celebrity avoiding paparazzi. Jack shuts the door behind us.

"What was all that about?" he asks but I ignore him and trot up the stairs. It should be obvious. I wait outside his flat on the balls of my feet, like a sprinter about to start a race, until he appears and then we're inside and I feel myself relax slightly. But not much because my mind keeps chasing down dark avenues.

Jack puts the kettle on. The great British tradition when in the face of adversity — get a cuppa going. He looks at me as the water bubbles, his face a question mark.

"If you must know, I'm shitting myself," I say. "The cops are going to be banging on that door any time soon. I need to find somewhere else to stay, somewhere they can't find me."

"What are you on about?" He looks at me as if I've lost it, which I have.

"They're going to believe I killed Hershey."

"Well did you?"

"No I fucking didn't! He was already dead when I got there."

"So there's nothing to worry about."

"My DNA will be all over the place."

"Really, I think you'll be in the clear."

"I need to pack."

"Look, if I can get someone to confirm whether the police consider it suicide or murder will that help?"

"Maybe," I say grudgingly.

"Then sit down and drink this." He forces a steaming cup of tea into my hand.

He picks up his mobile to make a call, but before he can dial out it rings.

"Hello?" he says. He looks puzzled. "Hello, is anyone there?" It sounds like someone speaks at last because he replies, "Jack Dean. Who's this?"

But the caller rings off as Jack shrugs and makes a call of his own.

Once it connects he says, "Hi, Em? I need your help."

I have an idea and borrow Jack's phone once he's finished. I've still got the grubby piece of paper with the eleven-digit number and the letter K on it.

Another Piece Of The Puzzle

Mr Lamb tapped Hershey's Blackberry thoughtfully on his chin, having just hung up on Dean. A quick web search popped up very little on him but what he had gleaned was gold dust: IT expertise. It tallied with what he'd found on Valentine's laptop.

Last night Mr Lamb had had his 'meeting' with Shoe and it had gone well. Finally he felt his conclusions were beginning to coalesce into future actions.

Konstantin flipped his phone shut. He put the gum back into his mouth, removed out of courtesy whilst he spoke to Josh. He chewed on the tasteless rubbery lump thoughtfully for a few moments, wondering what would be so vital as to require his help. Then he shrugged. It didn't matter really. He'd find out soon enough.

Here She Comes

"Fuck me." I say. Stunned doesn't adequately express the level of surprise I experience when she enters the room.

"You couldn't afford it," she says, and stares hard before turning to give Jack a quick hug and kiss on the cheek. She removes her peaked hat and drops it on the small table in the living area, such as it is.

I look her up and down, the blonde from the train, but dressed very differently. Gone are the classy clothes and subtle make-up, replaced with a rather starched Special Police Constable's uniform.

"It was you I saw in the hospital," I say, sure now.

"Uh-huh," she replies, all cool. Her expression says she's uninterested in satisfying my curiosity because it makes no difference to her. "I attended the scene of your little fight so I had to follow up with a sick note visit."

"And on the train."

She shrugs, her lip turns up a notch. She neither remembers nor cares.

"Emily's with the police," Jack says.

"I worked that out for myself," I say with heavy sarcasm.

"Do you want me to help you out of your little predicament or not?" She fixes me with a glare again.

"Yes. Please."

"Then stop being such a prick to Jack," she says.

"Okay, sorry. I'm just fucking stressed," I raise my hands in surrender. "I'm not used to finding dead bodies."

But before she can tell me (literally, her beautiful mouth is open for the words to exit) the doorbell rattles again.

"That's for me," I say. "Could you get it please, Jack? In case it isn't."

"Let the lazy shit get it for himself, Jack," Emily says.

"No, I don't mind," Jack says. "He's been through a lot."

"What happened to helping the public?" I ask.

He dutifully trots off. Emily turns her back on me, casting her Medusa's gaze on anything in Jack's tiny flat other than me. Her radio squawks a blast of static followed by a tinny voice. She grabs it and twists a small knob on the top so the volume drops right back to a barely audible chatter.

I can't believe it; here she finally is, in the flesh, in the same location as me. All those weeks of chasing a shadow only for her to turn up now, called by Jack of all people. However, I'm experiencing one of those 'be careful what you wish for' moments because I can hardly claim that my hopes are being met so far. My initial impression is that Emily's as hard as fucking nails, beauty with knuckles in the teeth.

My observations are interrupted by the door to Jack's little flat opening. Konstantin literally fills the room. His familiar odour enters alongside him, a malevolent companion that assaults my nostrils as effectively as pepper spray. Emily seems entirely unaffected by the olfactory mugging meted out by the tramp with dubious origins.

"Hallo, funny man!" Konstantin booms. He crosses the room and slaps me on the shoulder, sending me staggering as his ham-sized hand thuds down. He catches sight of Emily and his grip strengthens. "Who this beautiful lady?" he asks in mock reverence, like a priest confronted with a manifestation of his God.

"The police," she says in an icy tone meant to intimidate. It works on me but not on Konstantin, who simply booms with laughter again.

"She funny like you!" Konstantin says, obviously full of mirth today. He finally takes his hand off my shoulder and I can stand upright again.

"Can we just get on with this?" Emily directs this at Jack. "I've far better shit to do."

"Sorry Em, go on."

Emily looks down at her polished shoes for a moment, gathering her thoughts. "The top brass are all over this like herpes, even Davis turned up and took a look around apparently. I'll be in the shit up to my ears if anyone finds out I've told you anything so not a fucking word, okay?" She waits for each of us to nod in agreement, takes a deep breath and dives in. "Currently the senior officer in charge of the Valentine investigation has no reason to believe the cause of death to be anything other than suicide."

"Thank fuck," I say with relief.

Emily continues as if I haven't spoken. "The crime scene's been thoroughly swept and there's no evidence of anyone else's involvement, no fingerprints, nothing. There was a gun found at the scene but it only had the victim's dabs on. The wound and splatter pattern also indicates a self-inflicted fatality."

I remember the gore and involuntarily shudder. "So that's it, I'm in the clear."

"The evidence points to suicide as I said, not murder, so unless you know something I don't?" Emily says.

I back-pedal fucking quickly. "No. Why would I?"

"If we're finished here I have to go. My superiors think I'm helping an old granny across a street."

"Thanks Emily," I say.

She softens for the briefest of moments. "You're welcome," she says and then is out the door and gone.

"She's a hard one," I say to Jack.

"So would you be if you lead the life she does."

"What? Money, house, cars, holidays, marriage? Give me a break, Jack. That's pretty much what everyone wants."

"Her husband, my brother, doesn't give a shit about Emily. In fact I suspect he's gay. Em's just an asset to further his career. She's been hooked on alcohol and drugs and beaten both. She sleeps with any man that crosses her path and she lives this double life as Serena. First she was a strippergram, then a pole dancer, then an escort and the latest is branching out into porn, although she says she hasn't filmed anything yet."

"Christ."

"She's really the nicest person you could ever meet."

"How do you know all this?"

"I'm the only person she says anything to. My git of a brother isn't interested."

Konstantin sighs. "I bored of this shit," he says. "Now funny man, I have thing for you."

I've a hundred more questions for Jack, but I guess they'll have to wait. The train of conversation has been derailed.

"What thing?" I ask.

"Man who follow, the spy. Have photo."

Konstantin holds up his phone, a picture on the tiny screen. Of someone I thought I knew well, but clearly not at all.

"Holy shit," I breathe.

"He at American's house."

"Are you sure?"

"Da, I there too," Konstantin grins.

"And me," Jack says, looking downcast.

"Perhaps you'd better tell me what the *fuck's* been going on," I say.

So Jack does.

Welcome To Hell

Culpepper strode the length of the grim, dingy church to deliver his eulogy. It took hardly any time at all to cover the distance, the place was tiny. A week had passed since Hershey's death, during which time the police had completed the paperwork stating expiration was by his own hand and had released the body. There'd be an inquest, but it was expected to be a case as crystal clear-cut as one of Culpepper's whisky glasses.

In the interim Hershey's finances had been thoroughly delved into (by the police and by Culpepper). No will and no family could be found. Hershey did have a lawyer, as any half-powerful American would, and he revealed Hershey was flat broke. The grand house was rented (unsurprising) and his bank account yawned empty except for a few pennies. It appeared Hershey had lived a double life of extravagance (expensive meals out, holidays and clothes) and benevolence (a huge donation to a cat charity). The latter had surprised the hell out of the Culpepper. As a result of the paucity of Hershey's financial position the funeral was necessarily low cost — a ramshackle crematorium was all the budget would stretch to, because Culpepper was damned if the Bank would pick up the balance.

He reached the lectern, which was on the extreme right of the draughty rectangular area of worship. Front and centre was a cheap pine coffin, the lid tightly closed because of the damage to Hershey's skull. It sat on a conveyor, ready to be processed by the furnace that Culpepper imagined smouldered at the rear of the mouldy drapes, the gates of Hades.

Culpepper nodded at the nervous-looking vicar and wobbled up the two rickety steps to face the congregation, his elevation slight. The description 'congregation' was somewhat of an embellishment, however. Five people stared back at Culpepper, spread out across the little worship area of the building. They were Hershey's secretary Elodie, Mr Lamb, some computer guy he didn't recognise but claimed to have known Hershey (Culpepper had just shrugged whenever they'd met), a woman who had introduced herself as a PR consultant, but she was so plain Culpepper had

194

promptly forgotten her name, and a tramp on the back row who'd slipped in as everyone had taken their seats.

"Hershey Valentine was a highly valued member of our organisation," Culpepper said, reading from the first of two pages covered with densely packed script that he'd spent the days since Valentine's death honing. It had taken so long because he'd found it hard to be positive about someone he hated so much. "He contributed in more ways than it's possible to count. His friends were many and he was highly valued by his colleagues." He ignored the fact that few of his colleagues and none of friends were actually present. "He had an unusually analytical mind, highly capable of rooting out opportunities and capitalising on them." Strictly this was true, but Culpepper now knew them to be entirely self-motivated.

There was plenty more like this to come, but a quick glance up at the congregation and their highly sceptical expressions showed Culpepper his false words were known to be so. Even the tramp looked unmoved, a broad grin on his face, like Culpepper was in the midst of telling some great joke.

Which actually he was.

He looked back down at the script, opened his mouth to speak, but the words wouldn't come. They stuck in his throat like a fishbone. He balled up his fist, scrunching the paper into a lump.

"Oh, what the hell," Culpepper said, tossing the lies away and regarding the five people. "If truth be told there's very little, if any, good that can be said about Hershey Valentine. Frankly I didn't like him very much. He was a self-serving, lying little shit who only looked out for himself and lived solely off the reputation and hard work of others. Hershey was simply far more trouble than he was worth, and that so few of us are here to see him off is testament to that fact. Unless anyone else has anything else to say I suggest we burn his worthless bones."

Elodie stood up, three rows back. "I hated him. He treated me like a whore," she said, then returned to her seat.

"He told me I was worthless and friendless," said Jack, two rows back, "whereas now I know he was talking about himself, not me."

"Hershey showed me there was more to my life than I thought. He changed me utterly forever. But he lied to me, cheated me and cost me my job," said Claire, who sat to Jack's right.

As Claire slowly returned to her seat Culpepper looked to Mr Lamb, who just shook his head. Culpepper noticed the tramp slipping out of the door. Perhaps he'd got bored.

"Then on that note, why don't we get shot of him," Culpepper said. He nodded at the vicar who stood next to the lectern.

"Wouldn't you like me to say a few words?" the vicar said. He looked terribly young and rather awed by the Chairman, who shook his head.

"No point reverend. No one's listening up there."

Culpepper descended the two steps, which creaked with his weight. The coffin jerked its way along the conveyor belt as if it were a prize on a cheesy 1970's game show. He strode out of the worship area to the sagging doors at the rear without looking back and stepped gratefully into the daylight. Mr Lamb silently followed.

"Thank fuck that's over," Culpepper said. It was a short walk to the Jaguar, which already had its engine silently running and the door open to return him to the real world.

"Can you excuse me a moment," Mr Lamb said, his eyes fixed on something in the graveyard.

"I'm not hanging around this shithole any longer."

"As you wish."

Culpepper climbed into his car without another word. The chauffeur closed the door, got in himself and drew carefully away. Mr Lamb waited for the Jaguar to be completely out of sight before walking over to face the music of the damned.

Konstantin Misses Again

I watch Liam thread his way over to me, switching back and forth through the headstones. I wonder if he's the sort of person who avoids treading on the piece of turf above a body out of respect, or one who wades right through with utter disregard. As he nears my position, underneath a ratty tree, I'm surprised to see he's the former. He pauses a little more than an arm's length away from me and regards me impassively.

"Who the fuck *are* you?" I ask eventually.

"Not that it really matters, but I'm known within certain circles as Mr Lamb."

It's incredible, like a different personality within the same body. All Liam's restrained joviality is gone, he speaks in a quiet, balanced tone. His eyes are as sharp as a cat's and it feels like he's looking deep into me. He holds himself differently too, outwardly looking relaxed but with the tension of a compressed spring underneath. It's unnerving to say the least. He continues to stare at me with those blank eyes.

"I assume, by your association a moment ago, you're working for Culpepper."

Liam nods almost imperceptibly.

"What do you want from me?"

"Absolutely nothing. There's not a single thing you can offer me, I've everything I could ever need or want."

"Lucky you."

"It's absolutely nothing to do with something as frail as luck, I'm afraid. I'm just extremely good at making things happen for people in the way they want them to, and I'm paid extremely well to do so."

It starts to rain, softly at first but then with increasing severity. The tree offers scant protection and I'm getting very wet, but I can't draw myself away from Liam, or whatever his name is. He's not ready to go yet, either. There's clearly something he wants to say, but I have to pull it out of him.

"Did you kill him? Did you kill Hershey?"

"Categorically not," Liam says heavily. "I undertake many, ah, activities but not within that category."

"But anything else goes?"

"The activity depends upon the opportunity."

He draws a piece of paper out of his pocket and passes it to me. I hesitate a moment.

"I've already told you, I don't kill people. Not any more." A smile. I take the paper. He turns to leave but looks back at me over his shoulder. "Say hello to Konstantin for me."

I envelop the soggy paper in my palm and shove it in my pocket before it gets totally ruined. Liam stares at me a moment longer, nods and then strides away.

Konstantin suddenly appears beside me. I hadn't heard his approach. "Second time I no get chance kill someone," he says in a melancholic tone. In his hand he carries a suitcase within which I know, because he's shown me, is a silenced rifle.

"I said you were overreacting."

Konstantin shakes his head. "No funny man, impossible take anyone like him too serious. Coming?"

I shake my head. He shrugs and then I'm on my own, with more questions than answers. Perhaps the veil will lift if I go to the address on the piece of paper Liam has just handed me.

Disclosure

I'm where and when Liam suggested.

It's a grand old pile on the edge of the Cotswolds, some tiny little village called Conderton, a very exclusive enclave of houses solidly built in local yellow stone at the foot of Bredon Hill. It's quiet and dark, very dark, because there are no street lights in the village and none for several beyond either. It's like stepping several decades back in time.

The house I want is set back from the road behind high walls constructed of the same yellow brick. The gates yawn wide open but I choose to be discrete and go over the wall using an old yew tree whose mammoth branches extend out above the verge. Once over (which isn't as easy as I think) I pick my way through the undergrowth. The house is lit up like a Christmas tree so it isn't hard to find my way. The lawn is vast and flat as a bowling green. I stay in the shadows for as long as I can but as I near I see that eventually I'll have to be bold so I step onto the gravel drive, a sweeping affair that's as big as some people's gardens. The stones crunch underfoot. I cringe but no one challenges me. There are several decent motors parked at neat angles to the right of the vast front door, the carriages of the wealthy and influential.

The front door opens at my touch, the huge piece of ancient wood inlaid with iron handle and hinges swinging open silently and with surprising ease. I can hear faint voices, a sudden burst of laughter, deep in tone, and the clink of silverware on china. A dinner party then, men together enjoying something. I don't know Culpepper well, but I can't imagine a rave or a horde of dancing girls being his sort of do. Profound financial talk, heavy food, brandy and cigars are probably more like it.

I'm in a large hallway lit by electric wall lamps. There's a lot more wood, the walls, the floor and solid furniture are very traditional. A grand staircase twists up and away in front of me. In stark contrast to the dark oak there are works of art dotted along the corridor left and right, surprisingly bright modern paintings awash with colour. There are doors off the corridor, all closed. I want to know what's behind them because I've become mightily suspicious in recent weeks. So I explore, quietly opening one door after another — a study, a bathroom, a library stuffed with books and an airless living room that looks rarely used. All empty.

Back at the foot of the stairs another burst of distant laughter, deep and from the chest, comes from my left. I go up a level, keeping to the edge, but I freeze when one step rasps heavily and again when I lift my foot off. But still no one comes to investigate. I stretch my leg and step over the threatening creak. I reach the top of the stairs without any further mishap and poke my head into each of the bedrooms and two bathrooms, again all empty. It seems the only occupants of the house are in the party room. Perhaps Culpepper has given the servants the night off. Lucky them.

I turn right when my feet hit the bottom step, allowing myself at last to be drawn towards the noise. I can't delay any longer. Without pausing I enter the dining room. Three men are seated at one end of an extensive table. Culpepper is at its head holding court. The table is littered with china, cutlery, glasses (wine and brandy) and partially-consumed food. Smoke hangs in a pall over the table, adding to the feeling that this is some exclusive men's club. The three men all freeze, as if I've taken a photograph and etched their poses in time. Culpepper has a huge cigar clamped between two fingers an inch from his mouth, his lips pursed and ready to receive the butt. The others are holding glasses as large as bowls with a generous slug of a brown liquid within. I vaguely recognise one of Culpepper's dinner companions but before I can put name to face he catches sight of me.

"What the fuck are you doing here?" he demands, half rising out of his seat, hard eyes, grey hair and a physique that smacks of a relentless keep-fit regime. Someone who ordinarily would be more comfortable in a uniform rather than the beige cotton trousers, shirt and jumper affair he was currently wearing. Some people just prefer order and ties, you can tell the type.

Culpepper waves him down and the man reluctantly sinks into his seat, a scowl etched on his features reminding me he's the tough guy. The other man looks altogether softer. He's twisted in his chair to see me better. Younger than Culpepper, he has thinning hair, glasses and a greying beard. He sits awkwardly, as if he's too tall for the seating arrangement. He stays silent.

"Mr Dedman, how pleasant to see you," Culpepper smiles at me wolfishly, clearly not meaning a syllable of his platitude. "Would you like a cigar?" He waves a stogy at me that's the size of an average baby's leg.

"No I fucking don't," I say, to which Culpepper smiles all the broader.

"There's no need to be so uncouth Josh," says a soft voice from the far side of the room. "It's very much unlike you."

I regard the new entrant but don't say a word to avoid giving myself away.

"Mr Lamb works for me," Culpepper says, taking a large drag on his cigar and enjoying my falsified surprise. "He's my finest trouble-shooter."

Liam shrugs apologetically, closes the door then pads across the room to take his place at the table, confirming his membership of the select group.

"Ian!" says the hard-arse dinner guest sharply. "Be careful what you say."

"I'll say what I damn well please!" Culpepper glares at the grey-haired man and takes a large gulp of brandy from the goldfish bowl glass. He's either drunk or making very good progress at getting there.

"Now I know who you are," I say to the hard arse. "You're Davis, the Met's Commissioner."

"Rumbled!" Culpepper laughs, pointing the burning ember of his cigar at Davis, who glares back at him.

"But I don't know you," I say to the bearded man.

"Mr Lamb," Culpepper says, ignoring my deduction, "would you do the honours?"

Liam rises and walks towards me. I hold my ground. "Arms up, spread your legs," he orders in a tone that brooks no fucking about, so I don't.

"You are joking," I say. He isn't and subjects me to a rapid, but thorough, rummaging around of my personage.

"He's clean," Liam declares, stepping back from me.

"What, no cavity search?"

"Not even if you like that kind of thing. Christ, what do you think we are, perverts?" Culpepper smirks as Liam reclaims his place at the high table to the left of Jesus. Culpepper waves at an empty chair. "Take a seat," he orders.

I park my arse and look around the table at the disciples in turn. Bearded man refuses to meet my eye, finding something interesting in the wood grain no doubt. Culpepper affects a smug and arrogant expression as he eyes me back. Davis is simply a glare. Liam sits with his legs and arms folded, his body stretched out and eyes closed as if asleep or meditating.

"You haven't been introduced to Alan Levett here, have you?" Culpepper nods at the bearded guy who looks wide-eyed at being brought forcibly back into the discussion — like he's a rabbit and Culpepper a fast-moving car about to flatten him. "Alan is the Chief Coroner."

The penny drops with a thunk., though with the rate of inflation these days it's fast approaching a two pound coin.

"So someone to kill Hershey," I point at Liam (who still looks asleep) then move my accusatory finger to Davis, "someone to investigate the event and ensure only what you wanted to come to light was found and," — I sweep my digit to Levett — "someone to confirm the outcome you wanted. All very neat."

"You read too many detective novels," Culpepper says with a grin, then draws deeply on his cigar, making the tip glow bright for a couple of seconds.

"Rankin's my favourite," I say. Culpepper looks at me in a way that shows he doesn't have a clue who I'm referring to.

"Besides, I'm still £20 million down and the location of the money seems to have died with Mr Valentine," Culpepper says.

"Better to lose the money than lose the Bank's reputation?" I ask. Culpepper shrugs, but I can see I've hit a high note by the tick in his eye.

"Do you know where the money is?" Culpepper asks, leaning forward and poking the cigar at me.

I shrug. "Hershey loathed me and tried to set me up. He was hardly likely to tell me was he?"

Culpepper considers that nugget for a moment. A twitch and then a sharp nod of agreement.

"Why are you telling him all this?" Levett demands in the brief interlude, apparently finding some teeth behind that badly-trimmed shrub of a beard.

Culpepper shrugs. "It's his word against ours, four eminent men, all leaders in our field — well, except for you of course Levett — versus an unemployed slacker who has publically declared his hatred for the poor deceased Mr Valentine. And besides, I haven't told him anything. It's pure hypothesis and allegation on his part."

"Nevertheless it's time for this game to end, I think," Davis says forcibly. "There's nothing more to be discussed."

"That's a pity, just as I was warming to my subject," Culpepper pouts. "But you're probably right, Davis. Mr Lamb, would you care to show Mr Dedman off the premises?"

"I'll go to the newspapers," I say, albeit without conviction.

"You go ahead old boy," Culpepper grins. "As I've already said, you haven't a shred of evidence."

Which is true and we both know it.

"We'll be watching you," Davis warns.

"Is that a threat?"

Davis shakes his head. "Not at all. I just don't want you to have any nasty accidents. You wouldn't want Levett here poking around in your guts."

"Mr Lamb?" Culpepper says again.

"Come on Josh," Liam says, suddenly beside me. He grips my arm tightly and effortlessly compels me to rise. I'm half dragged, half pushed out of the room. I cast one last glance over my shoulder as we exit. Culpepper is smiling and waving goodbye, Davis is continuing to glare with stone cold eyes and Levett has his back to me again.

"Did you kill Valentine?" I ask Liam once we're in the corridor.

He ignores my question completely. "Where are you going to go Josh?"

"Go? Why would I be going *anywhere*?"

"Do you really think you can stay here now? After this? Culpepper will never leave you alone, I can tell you that for free."

He puts his hand into his pocket and keeps it there, which starts my heart racing. A gun perhaps? Another bullet to another temple? Another apparent suicide?

"What about you, will you leave me alone?" If he's going to kill me, we might as well get it over and done with.

"I happen to like you Josh," Liam says as we exit through the front door. Our feet crunch onto gravel.

"How nice, thank you," I try to be ironic. There's a light breeze on my face, bird song in the air, the smell of cut grass. Is this how it is when you know you're close to death? Suddenly everything comes into relief, your senses burst into life?

"I'll be retiring from my employment with Culpepper, this is my last job." Liam pulls his hand out of his pocket and my heart stops for a moment. I can't look down but I know Liam is pointing at me, something in his hand. A door unlocks with a clunk behind me making me jump.

203

"A fucking car key," I say, adrenaline dumping into my bloodstream.

"Of course, what else would it be?"

"True, what else?" I laugh with a tinge of hysteria.

"Take some advice for once, go somewhere far away and go soon. Things are going to get messy and you'll be glad not to be in the country."

"What are you going to do?"

Liam, Mr Lamb, grins. "Can I drop you somewhere?"

"No thanks, I'll walk."

No point being driven to my grave if he changes his mind or Culpepper calls, I think.

"Hope I don't see you around," Liam says, holding out a hand. Despite myself I take it and shake just once. His grip is firm, his palm dry as sandpaper. "I recommend somewhere warm and without an extradition treaty. Go and find someone."

Liam releases my hand, walks on a few paces and climbs into his car. He starts the engine and then winds the window down with a hum. "Oh, and Josh? Don't spend it all at once," he smiles again, each tooth an ice cube, and drives away without a backward glance.

"Fucking hell."

Ten minutes later and I'm in Jack's car doing forty miles an hour.

"Can't this thing go any faster?" I look in the wing mirror yet again, expecting Mr Lamb to come barrelling up the outside lane to put a bullet in the tyre. Just another accident statistic.

"Where are we going?" Jack asks, his mind too on the road to notice my anxiety, thank fuck.

A sudden thought strikes me and I smile. "Somewhere hot and far away without an extradition treaty." Jack glances at me with curiosity. "Just keep going south," I say.

Suddenly I feel a whole lot better. Life's pretty fucking excellent, in fact.

Epilogue
Alison

She answers on the third ring. Her voice is sullen. Like the cat that's got the cream only to find someone's pissed in it.

"Hello?" Claire says again, getting irritated. It doesn't take much.

"I'm sorry," I say.

There's a pause, an intake of breath. "Josh, is that you?"

"I just want to say that I'm not sorry, that's all," I say, then slowly lower the receiver into the cradle. I can hear her shouting my name all the way down, telling me it's all right and she'll take me back. Not a fucking chance.

I don't pause, don't reconsider. There's sudden silence as her voice is cut off with the connection. I'm safe in the knowledge Claire can't ring me back as call return doesn't work in Goa.

"Thanks," I say to Batiste, the owner of the bar we're currently profusely sweating in, despite the overhead fans. I hand him the phone, an old 1960s Bakelite model in cream.

He shrugs, as if it's no bother. "Another beer?" he asks. I shake my head. "Spliff?" I shake my head again. Batiste happens to sell the biggest joints you've ever seen but I don't need escapism right now.

I feel warm, inside and outside. I was going to apologise to Claire at first but as I put the receiver to my ear I changed my mind. After all, it wasn't me that had fucked other people, fucked me over or simply stood by when the shit hit the fan. However, perhaps it had been me that had put her in that place anyway. I'll never know, but I'll never feel bad again either.

I throw the approximately week-old newspaper in the bin (I don't wear a watch anymore so fuck knows what the date or time is). The front page continues to be dominated by a contagion called the credit crunch which has just claimed Northern Rock. Buried deep inside the broadsheet was a single column story of a similar ilk. Culpepper's Bank was down millions and evidence was emerging of dubious financial deals and holes in the accounts. A mole, one Edward Shoe, had blown the whistle. The Chairman's professional and personal life was unravelling fast. He'd been detained about to board a private jet allegedly bound for a small country that didn't have an extradition treaty with the UK. According to the report he was currently out on bail.

The column revealed another culprit, one Claire Pigeon, was suspected of having received at least £1m. Her character was neatly assassinated by a Ms. Hodges, her ex-boss at P&R PR, who stated 'nothing is beneath Miss Pigeon when it comes to ambition and greed.' Claire was also out on bail whilst further evidence was being gathered.

The rest of the missing cash, the theory went, had been siphoned off somewhere into a deeply hidden bank account by the now deceased Hershey. The stench of corruption was enough to drive the Bank's traditional customers away in droves. Of Liam, a.k.a. Mr Lamb, there was no mention. The article concluded that the remaining £19 million was likely gone for good.

Which is complete crap, of course. I know exactly where the money is.

Claire deserves all she'll get and £1m is a cheap price to pay to see that she does. We've also invested £1m in a company which makes and distributes lesbian porno films, of which Serena is the Managing Director. Konstantin, however, wouldn't take a penny, saying he'd had enough from me already, but the promise is there should he ever need it. I still have his number on that grubby piece of paper.

"Come on, let's go," I say to Jack, tapping him on the shoulder. He grins up at me, tanned and happy. We've a perfectly reasonable £18m to spend between us and in somewhere like Goa it'll last forever.

I wave to Batiste as we leave the bar. The heat hits me immediately we step outside. I soak it up, bathe in its warmth. I know I'll never be cold again. Now there's just one more thing to do.

Go and find Alison...

Lightning Source UK Ltd.
Milton Keynes UK
UKOW05f1332270214

227272UK00002B/5/P